Dear Reader,

Here's me at a recent Perfectionists Anonymous meeting: *Hi, I'm Dawn, and I'm a perfectionist…. No, wait, that's not quite it. I'm overly goal oriented…? No. Status quo challenged…? Nope. Capable of ironing my lingerie? Close…*

You get the idea. Been there, done that yourself? I hope so. Like Claire, I've made a few wrong turns in my life (and that's just finding the exit to my doctor's office) and I've learned to shrug and move on—or out, as the case may be. (Did you know a gynecologist's office can have seventeen different doors…some of which should definitely lock?)

Now, where was I? Oh, yes, perfection. I say, fugedaboutit. I just do the best I can to tell the stories of the characters who come to me in the night (many of them lost).

You know what helps a lot? Friends. My friends tell the best stories about me. Don't even think about asking them to share. I give reeeally expensive presents, so they'd never squeal.

Enjoy Claire's story and watch for my next book at www.dawnatkins.com!

Love and laughs forever,

Dawn Atkins

P.S. Please write to me—daphnedawn@cox.net!

"So, how about going out with me?"

Kyle was asking her out? Claire had definitely not seen this coming. He stood there looking uncertain what to say next.

He was kind of sweet. And, really, it was a good idea to get dating again. Maybe Kyle didn't give her a zing, but then she'd just broken up with the ex, so her zinger was still numb, right? And the over-the-top Trip zing? Champagne-induced, of course.

"Sure. We could do something," she said, rushing to ease his nervousness. "Anything you want. Whatever you enjoy."

"Oh. Well, I, uh, do have season tickets to the symphony."

"The symphony would be lovely." The *symphony?* Hello? The symphony was for blue hairs who toddled over after the early-bird prime rib special at Beefeaters. It was *mature*, though. And adult. And didn't she want a mature, adult life? This was exactly what she needed. The encounter with Trip had helped her move on. And now she could start a sensible relationship with Kyle. This could be perfect.

Too bad about the zing, though.

A PERFECT LIFE?

DAWN ATKINS

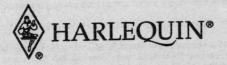

HARLEQUIN®

TORONTO • NEW YORK • LONDON
AMSTERDAM • PARIS • SYDNEY • HAMBURG
STOCKHOLM • ATHENS • TOKYO • MILAN • MADRID
PRAGUE • WARSAW • BUDAPEST • AUCKLAND

ISBN 0-373-44185-1

A PERFECT LIFE?

Copyright © 2004 by Daphne Atkeson.

This edition published by arrangement with Harlequin Books S.A.

® and TM are trademarks of the publisher. Trademarks indicated with ® are registered in the United States Patent and Trademark Office, the Canadian Trade Marks Office and in other countries.

Visit us at www.eHarlequin.com

Printed in U.S.A.

ABOUT THE AUTHOR

Dawn Atkins wanted to be a writer the minute she put fat pencil to thick-lined school paper. After years of being known for her "offbeat humor" (read "she's Looney Tunes"), becoming a published romantic comedy author made Dawn Atkins feel as if she'd come home...to the funny farm. (And she means that in a good way). After all, her likely response to her husband's and son's heartfelt "I love you," is "I love...cake!" What's love without laughter, she asks? And what if the Hokey-Pokey really is what it's all about? Dawn has been a teacher, freelance feature writer and a public relations person. She lives in Arizona with her husband and son.

Books by Dawn Atkins

HARLEQUIN TEMPTATION
871—THE COWBOY FLING
895—LIPSTICK ON HIS COLLAR
945—ROOM...BUT NOT BORED!

HARLEQUIN DUETS
77—ANCHOR THAT MAN!
91—WEDDING FOR ONE/
   TATTOO FOR TWO

HARLEQUIN BLAZE
93—FRIENDLY PERSUASION

Don't miss any of our special offers. Write to us at the following address for information on our newest releases.

Harlequin Reader Service
U.S.: 3010 Walden Ave., P.O. Box 1325, Buffalo, NY 14269
Canadian: P.O. Box 609, Fort Erie, Ont. L2A 5X3

To my editor, Wanda Ottewell,
who believed in this story—and me—from the start.

Acknowledgments

I love Phoenix—especially downtown—
but readers who know the area will realize that
most of the locations in this book are imaginary,
though they may be inspired by a real bar or
building. I hope I've given you an authentic feel
for the place. Ziggie's, by the way, is real,
and an absolutely terrific music store.

1

"So, Claire Quinn, it says on this card you're in love. That right?"

"Huh?" Claire pressed the phone to her ear and squinted at her bedside clock, wondering who the hell was calling about her love life at 7:15 a.m. This early, she hardly knew her own name.

"Frank and Phil here, Radio K-BUZ, double-eleven on your dial," the lush voice answered. "How are you this fine morning? On the one-week countdown to Valentine's Day."

"Asleep," she mumbled. "And you?"

"Oh, we're just fine. But not as fine as you're going to be."

"Why is that? And how did you get my name?" She never listened to K-BUZ, which was easy-listening elevator music for fortysomethings. She jerked to a sit. "Wait. Am I on the air?"

"You bet your sweet, um, *heart* you're on the air. You're on our Morning Madness Show, where you've been selected as today's 'Someone Loves Me' winner."

"I've been selected? I'm a winner?" She vaguely recalled her friend Kitty laughingly dropping Claire's business card into a fishbowl plastered with radio call letters at Vito's Bistro after lunch two weeks ago, when she'd first told her friend that she and Jared were in love.

Claire was not the radio contest type, but then she'd never been in love before, either, so Kitty's gesture had seemed the perfect ending to their lunch, during which Claire had talked nonstop—from the focaccia bread through the blackened mahi-mahi salads to the decaf mocha lattes and fat-free flan—about how Jared was the perfect man for her about-to-be-perfect life. Maybe not perfect, but you had to set your sights high, right?

"So you're in love?" Frank or Phil asked again.

"Uh, yes, I am," she said. "You bet." She was pretty sure. Who really knew about love? Everyone told a different story and none of it matched the movies.

Still, doubts and all, she'd just pronounced herself a woman in love to thousands of radio listeners. She wondered who had heard her happy news. Not Jared, who was back in Reno until Saturday, when he'd move into their perfect apartment in CityScapes, the brand-new building on Central Avenue, in which Claire had lived for five fabulous days.

At first it would only be part-time for Jared—he was only in Phoenix three days a week—but he'd look for a sales job here, she was sure, or transfer to the Phoenix office ASAP.

"Tell us what you love about this guy," the disc jockey asked.

"What I love? Um, lots of things." How romantic he was, how he focused on her—really focused—and made her feel vital to his well-being. That was powerful. "It's personal."

"Okay, if you're not gonna give us the juicy stuff..." Frank/Phil gave a theatrical sigh. "I guess we'll just have to tell you about your prize."

Hadn't she already won the best prize of all? True

love? On the other hand, overkill in the prize department was okay by her. "What is it?"

"Claire Quinn, you have won a Valentine's Day gift from the man you love, courtesy of K-BUZ Radio."

"Really?"

"Truly. Tell us his name, this master of love."

"Jared."

"How do you know Jared loves you, Claire?"

"Well, he told me so." And it had been perfect. He'd just blurted it out. And it had sounded so right that she'd said it back. And then there it was—floating in the air between them like a soap bubble. They were in love. And she'd been floating right along with the words ever since.

"He told you...sounds good. What other evidence do you have?" The DJ paused for her to say something clever or funny or romantic or profound. But all she could do was breathe into the phone. It was too early to even be conscious, let alone clever or funny or romantic or profound.

"Okay," the DJ said, sounding exasperated at her lack of showmanship. "Just give us his number and we'll tell him what he's won for you."

"You want to call him? But he's in Nevada right now."

"Not a prob. Give us the four-one-one. You just stay on the line and listen in. Don't say anything and we'll surprise him."

The phone rang three times and Jared answered sleepily. So cute. She loved when he sounded sleepy.

"This Jared?" Frank or Phil asked.

"Yeah. Who's this?"

"Frank and Phil, K-BUZ Radio. You're a 'Someone Loves Me' winner on our Morning Madness Show."

"I'm a what...? On the where? A winner?"

"Yes, indeedy."

"Is this for real? Am I on the air?"

"Yeppers. And you've just won a dozen roses to be delivered to the woman you love."

"You're kidding! Wow!" He sounded as excited as a kid. That was one thing about Jared that bothered Claire—his immaturity. He sulked when he didn't get his way and ducked any serious topics. He was sweet, though. The huskiness in his voice reminded her how gentle he was in bed. Not the most suave or exciting, but that was beside the point. The point was that he didn't sleep well when he wasn't wrapped around her. She loved that. So romantic.

She held her breath so Jared wouldn't know she was there. This was so great. If she'd had any doubts that she was doing the right thing, here was proof from the universe. Falling in love had earned her a prize. And just in time for Valentine's Day—always a sucky holiday for her. Maybe her friend Zoe, who was into woo-woo, was right about karma. And Claire's karma was suddenly coming up roses.

"So, Jared, who should we make the card out to?" Frank or Phil asked. "Who is the lady you love?"

Here it came. Jared would say her name to thousands of radio listeners.

"Make the card out to my wife Lindi. Lindi with an 'i.'"

Claire gasped. "Your wife?!" The floor seemed shift to the side and she felt dizzy.

"Who is that?" Jared asked.

"Your wife?!" Claire repeated, the words thundering through her. Jared was married? He had a wife?

Probably right there in bed next to him. In something filmy and pink. But maybe her legs weren't shaved.

"Uh-oh," Jared said, his voice filled with dread. "Claire?"

"You're damn right it's Claire," she yelled. "You're married? How could you? You prick!"

Frank and Phil's barely stifled laughter made her realize that they'd listened in on her betrayal, along with thousands of people out in radio land. Omigod!

Claire slammed the receiver on Jared's plaintive, "Let me explain," her face burning. She felt like one of those women on a TV special who was clueless that her husband was a bigamist. Her heart thudded so hard in her chest she thought her ribs might give way.

My wife Lindi. Lindi with an "i," for God's sake. She couldn't believe it. What kind of woman had the name Lindi? Some perky housewife who ironed her husband's boxers and made her own clothes.

A memory zipped through Claire's mind—Jared telling her he loved her, his eyes full of adoration—and then sizzled in the bug zapper of his last sentence. *Make it out to my wife Lindi.* No hesitation, no question who would get his love roses. How had Claire been so stupid?

But she hadn't been stupid. She'd read the *Cosmo* article, "Ten Signs Your Man is Married," and Jared had come out clean. His ring finger was as tan as the other nine. Sure, he'd given her only a cell phone number, but as a salesman he was constantly on the road, so a cell phone made sense.

Mixed-up emotions—shock, grief, disbelief, outrage—churned inside her like surf. The phone rang and she jumped at the sound, then picked up the receiver, her hand trembling.

"Let me explain, Claire." Jared.

For an instant, hope bloomed. Maybe it had been a mistake. April Fool's in February? "Is it true?" she demanded. "Are you married?"

"Yes, but—"

Bam! She banged down the phone. And instantly wanted to snatch it back. No, she should be strong, stay mad. Her gaze fell on the brass puffin Jared had given her as a move-in gift. She picked it off the TV tray she used as a nightstand and reared back to fling it across the room. Just in time she realized it would leave a big hole in the Navajo white of her perfect new apartment wall, so she slammed it onto the patterned Berber carpet instead.

The phone rang again. She lifted the receiver and dropped it. She had to think this through before she talked to Jared. She hurt all over—like an all-body toothache and she needed some air.

Rushing to the double-paned arcadia door that had kept the city clamor to a whisper while she'd slept, Claire tugged it open and stepped onto her bookshelf-size terrace. Sucking in fresh oxygen, she let Central Avenue's hum and growl fill her ears. For a second, she remembered how happy she was to be here—right in the middle of downtown, close to the city's pulse, part of the action. From the fifth floor, she could easily see Camelback Mountain.

What about the apartment now? This was Claire's first adult place and she was going to gradually buy real furniture, not the bricks-and-board shelves or bean bag chairs she'd had since college. Jared and she had been going to split the rent and on move-in day— Saturday—they were going to buy a couch together. Well, a futon, but close enough. Buying furniture was a committed couple thing to do. Except Jared was already committed to someone else.

That lovely bubble of love she'd been floating around in popped, splattering her with stinging flecks of soap, thanks to K-BUZ Radio's Valentine's Day extravaganza. Without Jared, she wouldn't be able to keep this apartment. Not without a huge raise. She was only a mini account exec at Biggs & Vega Advertising, with tiny clients—car repair shops, a tire wholesaler and dry cleaners—and it would take her a while to build. She'd just begun her buckle-down campaign a week ago. She was twenty-five—a whole quarter of a century old—with a serious boyfriend, she'd reasoned, so it was time to get serious about her career. Just the day before she'd asked Ryan Ames, a senior account exec, to be her mentor.

Her mind flitted through odd thoughts—her futon-no-more, her now-too-expensive apartment, her new mentor Ryan and Mr. Tires, her biggest tiny account—anything but the nuclear blast that had just vaporized her heart.

Maybe she was still asleep and this was a nightmare. She pinched herself on the forearm—*ouch*—and then again just to be sure. *Ouch again.* She was awake, all right. And filled with the feeling she got when she'd done something dreadful—like spilled red punch on Mr. Biggs's Italian loafers at the Christmas party or bit down on a walnut shell, cracking her tooth—situations where she'd give anything to do a quick rewind of the moment. Turn left instead of right. Spit instead of swallow.

She grabbed the railing and took in more air. Blindly, she watched traffic pass. How many people zipping down Central had just heard her on-air humiliation? Her gaze caught on a man heading toward her building. She recognized him as the musician who'd been playing on her corner for tips the last couple of mornings. She'd dubbed him Guitar Guy. She was certain that he hadn't been listening to K-BUZ. He was about her age.

Claire stepped back into her bedroom, slid the door shut and thumped her head on the cool glass a couple of times before dropping to sit on the floor. Resting her chin on her knees, she let a couple of tears slip down her cheeks and onto her shins. But just two. That was all the leakage she'd allow for that rat. *Jared, how could you be married?*

And how had she picked him to fall in love with? She'd taken her time, looked around, chosen very carefully. Oh, yeah. She'd very carefully picked out a cheating bastard.

Well, she couldn't sit here feeling sorry for herself. Heartache or no, she had a job to get to. And a career to boost. She'd feel better once she got moving. *Shine it on,* her friend Kitty would tell her. *Climb back onto that little red tricycle and pedal on, sister.*

Managing a smile at the thought, Claire tromped to the bathroom and turned the shower on ultra hot. She grabbed the loofah Kitty and her other two best friends had given her as part of their apartment-warming gift and dragged it across her back. Too scratchy. *No pain, no gain,* her friend Emily would say. She'd call the Jared disaster a learning experience. Zoe, who'd picked out the raspberry face soother, would tell her to be gentle with herself to get through the hurt.

Claire sighed. She needed to talk to her friends about this disaster. The four called themselves the Chickateers—all for one and one for all—sharing the good, the bad and the dreadful every Wednesday for Game Night. They gathered at Talkers, a bar not far from Claire's apartment, to talk, drink wine and play a game they took turns choosing.

Thank God tonight was Game Night. She would share her tale of woe and the Chickateers would tell her what to do. And it would all be okay.

Scalded pink from the sizzling shower, Claire wrapped herself in a thick Egyptian-cotton towel— also from the Chickateers—and headed for her huge walk-in closet—another thing she loved about this apartment and did not want to lose.

What to wear? Now that she was getting serious about her career, clothes were an issue. In advertising, appearance was everything. She had to make the right statement. She pulled out a Lycra tank top and suede miniskirt. Too casual. How about this kicky gauze tie-dye number? Too femmie. She flipped more hangers. At the back, she found the suit her mother had given her when she first got hired at B&V. Navy blue, tailored lines. Very dress-for-success.

Perfect, because from now on, Claire would focus on success. Without Jared in her life, she could stay late at work, take work home. Not that her piddly-ass accounts required much extra effort. Penny-saver ads and newspaper flyers mostly. She sighed.

That's what Ryan Ames would help her with. He was new to the firm, but a very hot exec who'd brought some top accounts with him, and she was pretty sure he liked her. When she'd proposed the mentor idea yesterday, she'd thought she detected a flicker of the man-woman thing on his face, but it faded so fast she figured she'd imagined it. She'd definitely talk to him today. Anything to distract her from the misery that kept rising in her throat like one too many Jell-O shooters.

Clothes on, Claire headed into her bright white, mel-amine-cupboarded kitchen for something to put in her stomach. There was nothing but Crystal Lite and celery in the fridge. Just as well. She felt like hurling.

For a minute she wanted to crawl back into bed, suit and all, throw the covers over her head and just cry.

No way.

She had to keep going—slog through the day until Game Night, when her friends would help her. She needed their guidance more than ever. Jared the Jerk was proof positive that her judgment was wonky. Where were her instincts anyway? In her butt? Somewhere the sun didn't shine, that's for sure. She was clueless about men. And lame about love. Rotten at romance? That had a ring to it. If she were writing a commercial about herself.

No matter what, she would not call Jared. Uh-uh. Regardless of how her fingers itched to hit speed-dial one. No way. She'd walk to work. Early. Better to keep moving and stay away from phones.

She jogged to the elevator, rushed across the lobby, pushed out the glass doors and rounded the corner, where she ran smack-dab into Guitar Guy.

"Oh," she said, backing up a step. "Hi."

She had to admit he was a hunk. About her age, she thought, and very tan. This close she could see he wasn't a druggie. He had intense gray eyes that seemed smart, not frantic and not a bit bleary. Shaggy black hair—too long—hung over his forehead, and he wore comfortable-looking cords and a gray muscle shirt, worn, but clean. A stylized yin-yang tattoo ringed his left bicep, and he wore a stud in one ear. He smelled of soap—Irish Spring?—and patchouli.

Watching his fingers on the well-polished guitar, Claire felt a little vibration shimmy along her nerves. The music was old-fashioned and torchy. Something you'd drink brandy and sniffle to in some smoky bar. And he was good. Very good.

As she walked past, he spoke, the words so soft they were like a whisper in her head. "You're trying too hard."

She stopped dead and turned. "I beg your pardon?"

"That getup you're wearing." He gave her a slow head-to-toe perusal. There was a little bit of sex in it, but it was more like a friend determining whether something fifty-percent off was really you or not.

"You're critiquing my outfit?" she asked.

He met her gaze steadily. "Just making an observation."

"Well, I have one for you then. *You* need a haircut."

He considered her words, then gave her a crooked smile.

What? Now she was trading grooming tips with a homeless guy? Why not? She turned and started down the street, feeling Guitar Guy's eyes on her. Or maybe she was imagining that. Hoping for it? Nothing like breaking up with a guy to make you want proof you were still attractive.

Claire plowed doggedly onward, ignoring the way her pumps pinched her toes and rubbed her heels. Her suit was as airless as a plastic bag. By the time she reached B&V Advertising, she had blisters and felt woozy from being overheated. Oh, well. At least she had something besides her breakup to focus on—survival.

She paused at the door to the office to brace herself for the inevitable cracks from the Morning Madness fans at B&V who, she'd bet, included Georgia, the receptionist. Prepared, she took a deep breath and marched inside, head up, chest out, heels stinging, sweat dripping, but looking successful. Or at least dressed that way.

Luckily, Georgia wasn't at the front desk. That wasn't unusual, since she deserted her post whenever the spirit moved her. But at least Claire got through reception without a jab.

Needing coffee, she made a beeline for the tiny kitchen...where she hit a K-BUZ listener jackpot—Georgia and her friend Mimi, the bookkeeper. Claire attempted a backward slink, hoping to escape unnoticed, but Georgia spoke. "Moonlighting on the radio, are you now?" she asked in her smoke-roughened voice.

"You heard?" Blush washed over Claire.

"Was that staged?" Mimi asked. "The call and all?"

"No, it was real," she said. *Vividly, excruciatingly real.*

Georgia looked her dead-on. "They bleeped out what you called him. Was it 'prick' or 'dick'?"

"Prick."

"Yeah, I'd say that's the best word for him."

"You look bad, girl," Mimi said, looking her up and down. "Kinda like you dropped your vibrator in the bathtub—all shocked and jittery."

Georgia cackled and snorted smoke. This was a no-smoking office, but Georgia didn't let anyone push her around. "Good one," she said, then narrowed her gaze at Claire. "How you doin' with it?"

"Hide the razor blades," Claire said with a lopsided smile.

"Don't sell yourself short, honey. You deserve better than that putz."

Georgia and Mimi were both forty, divorced and okay with being single. Claire envied them their self-sufficiency.

"At least you have a great story to tell," Mimi said. "I learned my husband was cheating by finding Victoria's Secret receipts in his suit coat. So cliché."

"Good point," Claire said, comforting herself with three sugars and real cream in her coffee. She turned to face the women, resting her backside against the counter.

"Those mechanicals are on your chair to copy," Georgia said.

"Great. Just what I need—a visit with Leroy the Letch." The man lurked in the copy room and lived for a pat, brush or slide against some female part.

Georgia cackled again. "If that man gropes me one more time, I think I'll have to...I'll have to..."

"What?" Mimi said. "Sleep with him?"

The three women burst into laughter. It felt good to Claire—kind of like a mini Game Night.

"Nah," Georgia said. "I can't sleep with him. Mouth breathers snore."

They laughed again.

"Thanks for the pep talk," Claire said, raising her doctored brew in a toast to the two women. She turned to go.

"One more thing," Georgia said.

"Yeah?" She turned, expecting something motherly.

"Lose the suit. You look like a stewardess."

Just the image she was going for. "Honey-roasted nuts, anyone?" she said. Actually, she could think of a pair of nuts she'd love to roast. With no honey involved...unless the nuts were suspended over an ant-hill. Hmm...

"Don't feel bad," Mimi said, shrugging. "If you don't try things on for size, you can't learn what works."

"Right," she said. The advice was good for life, as well as clothes. Except everything Claire tried on was either too tight, too loose or made her butt look big. She set off for her office.

Low on the account exec totem pole, she'd been squeezed into the cubicle between the copy room and the mechanical room that used to be a janitor's closet. Now and then, when the breeze was right, she caught a whiff of cleaning supplies. She'd grown to love the smell of Comet in the morning.

She picked up the ads from her chair and began her foray into Leroy the Letch Land. Moving quickly, she escaped with barely a breast brush.

The minute she sat at her desk, the phone rang. "Claire Quinn," she said into it.

"Don't hang up!" Jared.

She took in a quick breath, knowing she should do just that, but the phone felt Velcroed to her ear.

"I wanted to tell you a million times," Jared said, "but I knew it would hurt you and I'd rather die than hurt you."

She could hear tears in his voice. *Tears.* She couldn't help but be touched. And a little weirded out. "How long have you been...?"

"Married?"

No, a cheating creep. "Yeah."

"Three years. We just sort of ended up together."

A thought chilled her. "Do you have kids?"

"No, no kids. And we've grown apart. I didn't realize how much until I met you and fell in love."

"Right." She tried to sound sarcastic, but the word *love* softened her like a VCR case on a dashboard in summer.

"It's a relief that you know the truth. You have no idea how this was haunting me."

"You poor, poor dear."

"I know, I know. Of course you're hurting more than me right now. We can talk this all through on Saturday."

"Saturday?"

"When I move in."

"You can't move in. You keep forgetting—you're married."

"We need to be together, Claire. This thing between us is big. Just give me time to talk to Lindi." His words were as sweet and soothing as warm honey on Claire's sore throat.

"We'll work it out," he continued. "I know we will. And on Saturday we can buy that futon, and a lamp— even an area rug—just like we planned. Anything you want, baby."

Anything she wanted. *Baby.* She loved it when he called her that. She fought down the throb of hope that tightened her throat. *Hold it right there, you lying sack of pig parts.* She decided on a more civilized approach.

"How can I trust you?" she said. "You lied to me. Our whole relationship is a lie."

"No. My marriage is the lie. Our love is the one true thing I have. You have every reason to hate me, Claire, but please don't stop loving me. Please."

She was touched, of course, but she couldn't help noticing he sounded like bad daytime TV. Plus, the picture of roasting his nuts kept floating in her head.

"I want to hold you," he said. "I need you in my arms to feel okay in the world."

Now that line was perfect and she felt herself melt right into her pumps, blisters and all. Maybe it would be okay. Men had to get shocked into change, didn't they?

"I don't know, Jared. I have to think."

"Take a day or two, but never forget that I love you. We'll find a way to make this work. We have to. What we have is real and true." More bad dialogue. *Stop that*, she told herself. The man was professing his love and she was critiquing his performance? That was Claire, though. *Always with the smart remarks*, as her mother used to say. Sarcasm kept the pain at bay.

Claire glanced up to find Georgia wagging a finger at her through the glass door, like she was a puppy who'd widdled on the carpet. *Bad girl.*

On the other hand, a smack on the nose with a rolled-up paper was probably exactly what she needed. "I've got to go, Jared." She ripped the phone from her ear and dropped it onto its cradle. The familiar wish to snatch it back washed over her. She had trouble making decisions. Yes, no. Stay, go. Sheesh.

Georgia smiled at her. She'd pleased Georgia, at least.

Claire checked her watch. Seven hours and fifteen minutes until she could plop this burden into the soft and willing laps of the Chickateers. Thank God for Game Night.

2

AT EXACTLY FIVE-THIRTY, Claire stepped off the bus and entered the cool dimness and expectant air of Talkers for Game Night. She surveyed the happy-hour crowd of downtown singles, looking for who of the Chickateers was already here. Claire loved this place and this weekly event. Waning sunlight slanted onto the bar and washed over the toned, well-groomed professionals around the room who were flirting, commiserating and dipping wontons in peanut sauce.

She spotted Kitty Knight at the far end of the bar. Kitty being Kitty, she was with a man. She leaned toward him, swinging her wineglass lazily between two fingers, just this side of slutty. If only Claire had Kitty's flair. Of course, Kitty also had a model's face, a flamboyant personality and saline implants. Claire had neither of the first two and no interest in the third. But Kitty stirred up a room like no one else and Claire loved trailing in her wake.

Kitty would be philosophical about the Jared fiasco. Men troubles rolled off Kitty's back like water over bath oil. She called it the Zen of men—*Be the man and you'll get the man.*

As Claire got closer, she could see the guy was writing something in his Palm Pilot. Kitty's number, no doubt. Just before he left, Kitty gave him that flattering once-over that Claire had actually practiced in the mirror once, feeling goofy.

Kitty spotted Claire and slid off her stool for a hug. She smelled of something new—probably a perfume sample from *Vogue*—she liked to test out the new stuff before she purchased it—and her hug was the usual well-meaning but painful grab.

"Who was that?" Claire asked, tilting her head toward Kitty's exiting conquest.

"Investment banker with two first names," Kitty said on a sigh. "Arnold Oliver. New in town. When Rex is over." Rex was Kitty's boyfriend *du jour*, a personal trainer at a health club. Kitty gave Claire an up-and-down. "Oh, my gawd, it's Career Girl Barbie."

"It's not that bad, is it?"

"Not for a stripper pretending to be a librarian. Wanna see my Dewey Dec-i-mals?" Kitty said in Marilyn Monroe's breathy voice.

Claire laughed. "Who died and made you fashion cop?" Guitar Guy, Georgia and now Kitty had taken potshots at her new look.

"What are friends for?" She grinned, which made Claire smile, too. Kitty's zingers came laced with affection, so Claire never felt wounded. "Zoe's here," Kitty said, nodding past her.

Claire turned to watch Zoe Bellows head their way, her waterproof nylon pants hissing as she moved. Zoe zipped herself into the lives of her lovers like a second skin, taking on their hobbies and interests. Her current boyfriend was outdoorsy.

Zoe would be completely empathetic with Claire. She was into Tarot, numerology and breathing. *Inhale health...exhale toxins.* Unnaturally optimistic, too, but Claire craved her slow, full-body, patchouliscented hugs.

"Hey," Zoe said to Kitty, hugging her as best she could, since Kitty didn't have the patience for Zoe's lengthy embraces. Then Zoe turned to Claire. Just as Claire had hoped, the hug was long and gentle with a deep inhale, slow exhale. Soothing as a hot bath. Tonight, Zoe smelled of mint and banana sunscreen, instead of the usual patchouli.

Of her three friends, Zoe was the most likely to pick up on Claire's shocked-by-her-vibrator expression, so she ducked away before Zoe could get a good look at her face. Claire wanted the sympathy in one big wave, not three little ones.

"So, you're still seeing Mountain Man?" Kitty asked Zoe.

"We're training for a bike trip through Mexico."

Kitty shuddered. "What a way to ruin a foreign country—crouched over a bicycle, pumping your ass off. Let's get a booth and wait for Em." She led them to their usual spot at the back near the small stage where musicians occasionally played. They preferred it because it was quieter here.

"Is it Emily's game?" Claire asked, sliding onto the cool leather banquette. Zoe nodded. They took turns choosing, matching the game to the chooser's mood. They'd started with the chess and backgammon in the café's collection, and then moved to games they brought themselves.

Fifteen minutes later, the three watched Emily Decker push through the door in a chic pantsuit, trailed by her husband Barry, who held two shopping bags by their handles. Emily hustled to the booth, determinedly kissed each woman on the cheek, smelling of her personally blended perfume mixed with expensive car leather, then slid in beside Kitty.

Barry set the shopping bags at his wife's feet. "I'll pick you up in three hours," he said, then gave the rest of the Chickateers a weak smile. He probably saw them as evil witches stirring up trouble over a bubbling brew. After one Game Night discussion, Emily had declared him a flop at oral sex; after another she'd convinced him to propose marriage.

"We were shopping for a valance for the guest bathroom," Emily explained. "Later, I'll show you some swatches." Emily had quit her job at a bank and now devoted herself to fixing up the home in Scottsdale they'd recently bought. To Claire, she seemed bored. The Chickateers already had been forced to admire her choice in kitchen knobs and light-switch plates.

Barry was kind of a schlub, and yet Claire couldn't help thinking how great it would be to have a man willing to shop for something as mundane as a valance. What heterosexual man even knew what one was? Or cared? Jared, she'd thought. But she'd been wrong about Jared. Completely wrong.

"So what's the game?" Kitty asked Emily. She filled Emily's wineglass with the "cunning" pinot noir she'd selected for their first bottle. Kitty always chose the wine.

Emily took an eager sip and held up her glass. The other three joined her in their traditional toast: "All for one and one for all... No sniveling!" Except that's exactly what Claire would be doing tonight.

Emily reached into one of the shopping bags and lifted out a board game, which she set on the table. "Voilà!"

"'Life'?" Kitty asked in amazement. "You brought 'The Game of Life'?"

"Yeah. Isn't it perfect? It was in a toy-store display window and I couldn't resist. I loved playing this as a kid. Choosing my career, earning my paycheck, getting married, putting the little pink and blue kids in my car..." She opened the lid as she talked, laid out the board and began to separate the money denominations.

"The Game of Life." How ironic, since Claire seemed to be losing her own private version. All messed up with love and uncertain at work, with an apartment she could no longer afford. So much for her perfect life. The bright, cheery game board blurred as her eyes filled. *Enough with the self-pity, already.* She ducked her nose into her wineglass to hide.

"Pick a car color. I'll be yellow," Emily said, shuffling the career and income cards.

Kitty grabbed the red car and Zoe said, "Green or blue, Claire?"

Claire couldn't speak, and a single fat tear plopped onto the table.

"What's wrong?" Zoe turned to look Claire full in the face.

Claire would be strong about this. She brushed the water from her cheeks and lifted her chin. "A demonstration," she said. She picked up the green car and inserted a little pink person into it. "Here's me, right?" Then she took a little blue person. "Jared goes here, right?" She started to put it beside the pink person, then stopped. "No, because he's already here." She stuck the blue token into Emily's yellow car. "Jared's married."

"He's what?" Zoe exclaimed, sucking in a breath.

"No!" Kitty and Emily said, jaws sagging like in a bad comedy sketch. The three friends looked from Claire to each other and back...twice. Their shock made her feel loads better.

"But, I thought Pinkie was moving in with you," Kitty said. Over one too many Fuzzy Navels, Claire had once mentioned that Jared's penis was a pinkish color and Kitty had seized on it as a nickname.

"How did you find out?" Emily asked.

"A radio call-in show."

"No!" all three said at once.

"Oh, yes." She told them the whole K-BUZ debacle, gratified by their horror and anger on her behalf. "So, Happy V Day to me." She took a drink of wine.

"Screw Valentine's Day," Kitty said. "It's just a plot by the jewelry industry to soak men for big bucks and make single women feel like roadkill."

"I'm so sorry, Claire," Emily said. Emily's advice would be practical and down-to-earth, which Claire valued, even if it came via bulldozer, aka, Emily's way or the highway.

"I really thought he loved me," Claire said.

"I'm sure he does love you." Zoe pulled her into her banana-paba-smelling arms for a quick hug. "He's just a little...well...mixed-up."

"Well, duh," Kitty said.

"Did he explain himself?" Zoe asked.

"His wife and he have grown apart. He didn't realize it until he met me."

"And started getting regular blow jobs," Kitty added.

"Kitty!" Zoe said.

"It's true. I bet Lindi-with-an-i hasn't delivered since she got him to say 'I do.'"

"It's more than that," Claire said, though Jared did seem stunned and grateful when she performed that particular act. "Anyway, he says we can work things out."

"And of course you told him to go piss up a rope," Emily said.

Claire didn't answer.

Kitty shook her head and tsked. "I wish you'd help yourself the way you help us."

Claire felt another tear escape and roll down her cheek.

Zoe hugged her again and they all remained supportively silent while Zoe frantically patted Claire's back. And patted.

When she felt welts forming, Claire gently extracted herself. She blew her nose on the tissue Emily proffered, forced a watery smile and lifted her wineglass in a toast. "Come on. No sniveling!"

"You just snivel away," Zoe said. "This is a special occasion. Right, girls?"

The four clinked glasses, then took a solemn drink in Claire's honor.

"What do you want us to do to Pinkie?" Kitty demanded, her eyes gleaming in the golden light. "Blow his cover with Lindi-with-an-i? Slash his tires? Trash his apartment?"

"Kitty!" Zoe said. Zoe kept trying to tone Kitty down, but they all knew it was no use and loved her for trying anyway. And Kitty for refusing to change.

"It's the company's apartment," Claire said gloomily. "He was going to move in with me on Saturday, remember?"

"So, we graffiti the walls. He'll be responsible for the damages," ever-practical Emily said.

"Yeah, baby. That's the ticket!" Kitty said. "Nobody messes with our crew." Kitty jutted her chin and thrust out her chest in a seated strut.

Claire felt a stab of satisfaction at the idea—and a rush of gratitude for her friends.

"That would be bad karma," Zoe said. "Negative energy boomerangs. And besides, maybe he'll leave his wife."

"You think so?" Claire asked more hopefully than she felt.

"Forget it," Kitty said. "Men who cheat want to have their cake and eat it, too."

"But maybe Jared's different," Zoe said.

"They're all different until they get what they want," Kitty said to Zoe, then patted Claire's hand. "Speaking of which, wasn't Jared splitting the rent on your apartment?"

Claire nodded. "I can't really afford it without him."

"Not to worry," Kitty said. "I'll move in with you."

Claire gulped. "But you just moved into that great duplex...."

"I've barely opened a few boxes. The landlord's driving me nuts already—whining about my music and the water bill. Life's not worth living without a daily parboil and loud tunes. Besides, that place isn't really me."

"What about your lease?"

"She'll let me out of it. Trust me. Deposit and all."

"But, you're kind of a night owl, aren't you?" Claire protested weakly.

"A night owl?" Kitty gave her a steady look, her mouth tight. "Don't worry. If *Thor* and I are going to get out the whips and leather we'll go to his place."

"You're seeing a guy named *Thor?*"

"She doesn't mean literally, Zoe," Claire said. "I'm sorry, Kitty." She knew that under her friend's hard-candy coating lay a marshmallow center. "I didn't mean anything by that."

"Eh, forget it. My moving in will be good for you. I'll introduce you to some new men and you'll forget all about Pinkie."

"But I thought Pinkie—I mean, Jared—was the one."

"There are lots of *ones*," Kitty said. "It's like a deli where the men take a number and every day we start over with number one. Rex knows some single guys. Don't worry."

Soon the four Chickateers were toasting the new roommates, and Claire began to woozily welcome the idea. Kitty would help her be strong. A tiger didn't change his spots or a rat his whiskers. With Kitty as a reality check, she'd be less vulnerable to Jared's soap-opera pleas.

When it was time to leave, Barry and Emily dropped Claire at CityScapes. The building that had seemed exciting and full of possibilities the day before now seemed hollow and lonely—and expensive. She trudged up the stairs, rode the elevator in sadness, plodded down her hall to her door...

And found an impossible surprise. Resting in front of her door were a dozen red roses, bright as blood. The typed card said, "To my dearest love. Jared."

She picked up the roses and pressed her face into their velvety softness and dusky perfume. She was Jared's dearest love. Her heart warmed...then turned to ice. She might be his *dearest* love, but she wasn't his *only* love. Lindi-with-an-i was going to get her own dozen blood-red roses next week, courtesy of K-BUZ radio. Claire stomped through the apartment, opened the window and tossed the roses out.

An hour later she was plucking the bright blooms from where they'd scattered in the newly planted hedges of her building. They were *roses*, for God's sake. Even when your boyfriend turned out to be a rat, you deserved a little beauty, didn't you? Especially a week before Valentine's Day. Hugging the flowers to her chest, Claire knew exactly how to think of them: a lovely parting gift.

TRIP OSBORN packed up his guitar, sorry that he'd missed the lively brunette who'd crashed into him yesterday. Her name was Claire, he thought—someone had called to her the first day he'd played on this corner.

She'd caught his eye from the first moment with her forward-leaning stance and bouncy walk. She looked his age, but seemed younger somehow. She was certainly more driven.

He wondered how she was doing today and what she was wearing. Yesterday, she'd marched down the sidewalk in a business suit and punishing shoes, upset as hell. Her brown eyes had been watery, her nose pink and she'd slumped instead of bounced. He'd had the urge to protect her—as if from oncoming traffic.

You're critiquing my outfit? He smiled to himself, remembering the jab. She had an edge to her. And maybe she was right about the haircut.

He'd get a tip on a good barber from Erik Terrifik, the blues giant he was taking class with. He'd come to Phoenix because of Erik and the visiting philosophy professor whose class he was taking at ASU.

He was sorry he'd missed a morning exchange with

Claire, but he'd better head to the neighborhood dive Erik owned. The place didn't open until later, but he liked the old-smoke-and-stale-beer smell of it. Atmosphere meant a lot in music. And life.

Trip had spent most of the years since high school in the West. He liked the open feeling, the sense of limitless possibilities. Long straight stretches of highway, winding mountain roads. And all the climates he could want, from baking Sonoran desert to high, cool Rockies.

In the smoky dimness of *Chez Oui*, while he waited for Erik to finish up with the beer delivery guy, Trip found himself thinking about the woman again. Claire. She had pretty eyes. Mink dark with flecks of milk chocolate. Smart eyes. And an expression both vulnerable and sturdy.

That was a lot to notice in a few passing glances and one quick collision, but he was good at reading people. You learned that in foster homes. You quickly figured out what counted, because things always changed, got lost or showed up out of the blue. You learned what to hang on to, what to fight for and what to shrug off, and always to be ready to move on. Lessons he maybe got too young, but good ones all the same.

He didn't blame his mom too much. Hadn't really at the time. She'd done her best. She was just...limited. He visited her whenever he blew through Colorado. She always baked him something awful. And he always ate it like it was gourmet.

He picked up the bar phone to sign up with a palm-trimming crew to make enough money for the next couple of months' rent at the guest house where he was staying. The work was dangerous—climbing hun-

dreds of feet in the air to work with sharp blades—but
that was why it paid so well.

Plus, he liked variety. He never stayed long in any
place or at any job, choosing both for the opportunity
to learn...about people, ideas, music and himself. He
liked college towns, so he could take classes from people he admired. Gigs were easy to come by near uni-
versities. Gig money paid his tuition. But he was happy
to work in restaurants or bars, on yard crews or as a
handyman to make his daily wage.

Just as he hung up the phone, Erik slid onto the stool
beside him, his guitar in hand. "'Sup?" he breathed in
his rumbling bass.

"Not much." Trip said, smiling at his teacher.

"You're wearin' that look." Erik winked at him.

"Yeah?" Trip opened his guitar case and removed
his baby.

"Yeah. The look of a cat after a big slurp of cream."

Trip chuckled. Erik was smart and wily, and the best
guitarist he'd had the privilege to know.

"It's a girl, am I right?" Erik said, fingering his
strings.

And he was intuitive. "Could be." Trip plucked
through a tune-up.

"So tell me about her."

"She's pretty. Nice eyes. Brown." He sighed.

"Uh-huh." Erik began to play Van Morrison's classic
"Brown-Eyed Girl." "I ain't heard ya talk about a
woman since you been in town."

Trip shrugged, then started up a harmony line to the
tune. "I like spending time on my own."

"My ass. You're jus' too lazy to call any of 'em."

Trip shrugged again. There had been women who
let him know they were interested, but none had

caught his eye. Except this Claire. Maybe because she was different than the women he usually spent time with. Which made her off-limits completely, of course. He moved into the chords he'd been learning from Erik, who'd stopped playing to muse a while.

"Women love musicians," he said. "I was always gettin' busy in the old days. But once I moved out here, Sara got her hooks in me.... You want to make that a minor seventh."

"Right," Trip said, adjusting his fingering.

"You probably think you'll never want to stick to a place, but there's a good side to it. A steadiness."

"I like variety."

"Watch that chord. Keep the arch and it'll flow easier."

"Yeah. Got it...."

"There's a joy in learning all one woman's tricks."

Trip didn't reply.

"I've got a gig on Tuesday if you want," Erik said.

"Sounds good." He reached for the new chord. And got it. He loved that feeling. Music was the best companion.

Erik gave him the details about where and when they'd be playing. "I could keep you busy if you'd stay around. You going after this brown-eyed girl?"

"Too much trouble."

"But that's the best kind of woman," Erik said, cackling. "The ones that are trouble."

"I don't think so." Trip didn't like disappointing people. He'd stayed some months in Denver for a woman, but she started getting on him about the future and his plans, and he'd itched to be on the road. It was always easier to think, to learn, to be himself when he kept moving.

She'd reminded him of Nancy, the girl he'd been
with during that mess with his final foster home. He'd
fallen hard and when she broke it off, he'd been
wrecked. But she'd pointed out what he needed to
know about himself and he'd never forgotten.

"So you say," Erik said, nodding and smiling his
wise Buddha smile. He strummed something so complex that Trip had to work to follow it. Good. He'd
rather focus on music than women any day.

"So, I GUESS YOU GET the master bedroom," Kitty said
to Claire Friday afternoon as they stood in the narrow
hall of Claire's apartment. When she'd said Kitty could
move in, it had never occurred to Claire that her own
bedroom might be up for grabs.

They'd agreed today was a good day for the move,
since Rex had the day off and could muscle her stuff
upstairs.

Barely moved into the duplex, Kitty hadn't had
much to pack. She'd boxed up her kitchen and bedroom stuff, emptied her closets and rented a truck yesterday. Kitty moved fast when she wanted something.
She and Rex had loaded the truck last night and now,
Rex was dutifully trotting Kitty's bed frame through
the front door.

"I guess you could pay less rent for the smaller bedroom," Claire offered.

"No, no," Kitty said, tapping a French-cut fingernail
on her lip, wearing her real-estate-deal look. "Having
the bigger bedroom will be like a finder's fee. You
found the place, after all, and paid the deposits."

She gave her an abrupt, bruising hug. "I'm sooo glad
we're doing this. We'll have so much fun. We can do

each other's makeup, drink wine and dissect men all night."

"Sure," Claire said, trying to look on the bright side of the situation. Kitty wouldn't let her mope about Jared, that was certain. Plus, a pint of ChocoCherry Rumba Swirl shared seemed way less sinful than one shoveled in alone.

"It'll be just like college," Kitty added.

"Uh, yeah." God, she hoped not. Claire had spent many an evening studying in the library so she didn't have to listen to Kitty's headboard thump against the other side of the living room wall. At least the apartment walls here were thick.

"That room," Kitty said to Rex the Robust, directing him to what they'd agreed would be her bedroom. The two women followed him inside to watch as he bolted the bed frame together. Just watching his muscles ripple from butt to ankle gave Claire thoughts.

"Gonna be tight," Kitty said.

"Huh?" Claire startled from her fantasy.

"The bed," Kitty added.

"Oh. Yeah. The bed." The frame did nearly cover the floor.

"Big bed," Rex said, rising to stand between them, his face red from exertion.

"All the better to amuse you with," Kitty said to him, scraping a finger through the stubble on his jaw.

"Really?" Rex said, catching Kitty's hint. "Great! I'll get the mattress." He barreled down the hall, like a kid who'd abruptly gotten permission to buy a video game.

"He's completely tireless in bed," Kitty said to Claire. "Like a machine. All muscle, all the time."

"Sounds nice." Simple and satisfying.

"Oh, it is. And don't worry. He has a friend—Dave, from the gym—who will be perfect for you."

"It's too soon to date, Kitty. I'm not over Jared."

"This isn't a date, Claire. This is getting laid. Bodily function...healthy release." Her words slowed at the end because Rex had come in with the mattress across his back, looking like Atlas holding the world. *All muscle...all the time.* Hmm.

"I've got to get ready for work," Claire said. "Let me know if you need anything else."

"I think I've got everything I need right here," Kitty said, not taking her eyes off Rex.

In the shower, Claire wondered why she couldn't think of sex as easy breezy as Kitty did. Why did she have to pick at it like a scab? *What does it mean? Where is it going? Will we get serious? Is he the one?* Why did she have to want it to be perfect?

Because when it went bad, it went very, very bad. Her mother hadn't been the same after Claire's dad left her for his secretary when Claire was sixteen.

Maybe that was why it was so hard for her to decide about men—she didn't want to make a mistake. She'd thought her parents were perfect and look what had happened. Plus, she could always see both sides of a situation. Each parent blamed the other for the break up—and the bad match they'd made in the first place—and wanted Claire to side with them. She'd somehow managed to keep them both happy.

Kitty was right about sex, though. Claire *should* think of it as a healthy release, like jogging or doing aerobics or taking a yoga class. Exercise was good for *all* your muscles, right? She would at least try Kitty's idea. Maybe with this Dave guy.

The idea sounded empty now, but after a few days

of celibacy, she was sure it would appeal. She should put in some time with the Thigh Buster, just in case. A weightlifter would be fussy about the legs he tangled with.

So, she was moving forward, making decisions, being clear. *Good girl*, she told herself, drying off. She'd forget about Jared, get casual about sex and serious about work.

In the closet, she faced another dressing quandary. That made her think of Guitar Guy calling her outfit a *getup* and she smiled. What should she wear? Forget the trying-too-hard suit. How about professional separates? A plaid skirt with a navy blazer. Conservative, but not so coffee-tea-or-me.

For shoes, she needed those damned navy heels again. She slapped a couple of adhesive patches over Wednesday's still-angry blisters—she wouldn't let a minor injury slow her down—and headed for the kitchen.

One good thing about having Kitty as a roommate was that she added cool stuff to the kitchen—a combo coffee-espresso maker, an industrial-grade blender and gourmet food. Claire scooped a spoonful of paté out of a plastic tub Kitty had plopped into the refrigerator and ate it. Mmm. Expensive protein. She'd read somewhere that protein eased depression. Or maybe that was only turkey, not duck liver. Duck liver probably depressed you because you realized you could never afford it on your salary...sigh.

On her way out the door, Claire paused to survey the living room. Even as her heart had emptied out, her apartment was filling up. Rex had placed Kitty's zebra-striped sofa where Jared's commitment futon had been slated to go. And beside it was a leopard-spotted chaise with pillows shaped like lips and a glass coffee table on a black lacquer base. Propped against the wall were a couple of paintings of abstract nudes from a former lover of Kitty's. The place was beginning to look like a singles pad. Not exactly Claire's style, but fun. Definitely fun.

She called a farewell to Kitty, who probably had her mouth too busy to reply, and hurried outside, pleased to see the bus hadn't arrived. Standing beside the bus bench, she shifted her weight from foot to foot, blisters throbbing slightly through the bandages, looking down Central.

"You were right."

The liquid voice came from behind her. She turned to see Guitar Guy, wearing jeans, a snug black T-shirt and his guitar. He looked better than the other day, and when he brushed back a strand of hair, she realized it was shorter.

"You got a haircut," she said.

"Yeah. I took your advice." He gave her a crooked smile, then tilted his head, indicating her body. "But you didn't take mine."

"Excuse me?"

"The nuns make you dress like that?"

She looked down at her skirt. God. He was right. The blazer and plaid skirt did seem like a Catholic school uniform. She shrugged. "All my idea, sorry to say. Maybe I should go change...." She bit her lip.

"Don't ever change," he said in mock seriousness.

She laughed. "You're just full of advice, huh?"

"That's why I get the big bucks."

"You'd probably make more money in Scottsdale. Lots of tourists."

"Too snooty. I like downtown people."

"Really?" Did he mean her?

As if in answer, he launched into the Billy Joel classic, "Just the Way You Are," a song about not changing to please him.

He was flirting with her. She grinned. Except maybe he just wanted her to tip him. But if he *was* flirting, a tip might insult him. Her instincts said he liked her, but where had her instincts gotten her so far? In love with a married schmuck.

The bus arrived, saving her a decision, and she climbed the steps. While the driver looked at her pass, she glanced out the door. Guitar Guy saluted her as the bus doors shut. He liked her. And his voice stayed in her head all the way to the office.

Inside B&V, Georgia and Mimi stood at the receptionist desk. "So let him *think* you're a lesbian," Georgia was saying. "Men *love* lesbians. They want to convert you. Plus, they think they have to be re-e-ally good at oral sex."

Mimi looked unconvinced. They both looked up at Claire.

"Well, lookie here," Georgia said, leaning over the reception counter. "Muffy's stopped in on the way to her tennis match."

"Oh, for cripe's sake," Claire said. "I give up." Catholic school or prep school—either way it was a bust. Despite what Guitar Guy had said, she should have changed clothes.

"Mr. Tires called again. He thinks the radial in the ad looks like a glazed doughnut."

"Great." The man spent no money on his tiny newspaper ads, but he wanted new creative every week. Small flippin' potatoes. She saw that Mimi held a folder with Ryan Ames's name on it.

"I'll take that to him," she said, tugging it from Mimi's fingers. She needed to schedule their first mentor meeting anyway—her first step up the career ladder.

At Ryan's office, she saw through his glass door he was reading the paper. She tapped. He frowned at the interruption, but when he saw it was her, smiled.

"Hi," she said, entering. She handed him the folder.

"Thanks." He smiled again. A big smile. A too-big smile. A definite man-woman smile. "So, how's my mentee doing so far?"

"Just great." Well, except for that broken heart, ruined life thing. "I was hoping we could get started on some strategy for me," she said. "Maybe over lunch. I'll buy." Paying for lunch was a power move, she'd read.

"You'll buy, huh?" *Isn't that cute?* his smile said. "For now, why don't you have a seat and we can get to know each other better." He patted the chair kitty-corner to his desk, tugging it closer to him.

Oh, ish. Claire sat delicately on the edge of the chair, then pushed it back a couple feet.

"You settled?" he said, resting his hand on her arm as if to steady her. Gross. The man was hitting on her.

"I'm fine."

"So, tell me about yourself," Ryan said, leaning forward.

She pushed back a bit farther. "There's not much to tell except I want to get ahead here." She would make sure he knew she wasn't interested in putting in any couch time to get there. "I want to prove myself through my work, of course. On my own merit. But I hope you can advise me where to concentrate my efforts. My *work* efforts." That couldn't be more clear.

"Sure, sure," he said, smiling. "We can talk all about

that over lunch. How do you stay in such good shape?"

"How do I...?" Blech, puke, retch. She had to nip this in the bud. "Tae Kwan Do," she blurted. "Black belt, with a specialty in self-defense."

"Oh, really?" Ryan's brow lifted in surprise.

"Absolutely. I can make a guy walk lopsided for the rest of his life."

"Well. That's impressive. I guess I know who to take with me when I cross a dark parking lot at night." He seemed to find her amusing, not life-threatening.

"So, how about we start with your top ten tips at lunch?" she said.

"Sure. Sounds good," he said, smiling. "But I've got the first tip for you right now?"

"Really? What is it?" This was a good sign.

"Quit dressing weird. You look like a hooker dressed as a schoolgirl."

"Check," she said, pretending to make a mark on a pad. Yet another fashion expert had weighed in on her style statement. "So, I'll meet you out front at noon for lunch and more tips?"

"Sounds good," he said, his words tinged with man-woman energy, despite her hint that she could cripple him. Why did everything have to be more complicated than it seemed?

3

On Saturday morning, Claire was in the kitchen eating granola and staring morosely at Jared's false-promise roses, while Kitty and Rex did Tae-Bo in the living room, when Mitch the doorman called up to say she had a delivery downstairs.

She figured it must be an apartment-warming gift from her mother, but when she stepped out of the elevator, she stopped dead in pure shock.

There in the middle of the lobby sat Jared on a cream-canvas futon. "Ta-da!" he said, gesturing at its puffy expanse. "Perfect, huh?" He beamed at her with that sweet, boyish look he had—sometimes charming, sometimes annoying. Right now it was both. "Come try it out." He held out his arms to her.

For just a second, she was tempted to comply, but this was one gift horse—rather, rat—she had to look straight in the mouth. She wasn't about to hug him. "What are you doing here?" she demanded.

"Moving in, of course. Here's the futon and here are my clothes," he said, indicating two big roller suitcases, as if that proved his intentions were good.

"What about your wife? Did you talk to her about us?"

Jared's eyes flicked away from her face for a second, telling her all she needed to know. "I told her I had concerns."

"Concerns? Jared, *I want a divorce* is way more than concerns."

"Important things take time, Claire. Everything's not black-and-white like you always want. At least I'm here and I can move in."

"No, you can't. I already have a roommate." A roommate who was probably doing the deed right now in what would have been Jared's office.

"How did you get a roommate in three days?"

"Kitty's got moving down to a science."

"But what about me?" He seemed completely confused.

"You snooze, you lose. I can't afford this place by myself. You were out, so Kitty was in."

"I told you I wanted to work this out. How could you?" He let his head fall back against the futon, looking crushed. The weak part of her wanted to run upstairs and say, "Everybody out. Back to plan A." But no way could she fold. Jared had a lot of promises to make and keep before she would take him back.

After a few seconds of sad sighs, Jared sat up. "You're right. I deserve this. I have to prove myself to you. I'll get another couple months at the company digs." He smiled sadly, his eyes saying, *Kiss me. I've earned it.*

For a second, he morphed from cheating bastard to repentant boyfriend, but she fought the urge to fall into his arms and forgive him. "Just tell your wife, Jared. We can't be together until you do."

"Why do you have to be so extreme?" he said.

"Insisting my boyfriend is single is extreme?"

"You know what I mean," he muttered. "What am I supposed to do about the futon?"

"I'll help you load it into your truck."

"We could put it in the apartment...kind of a down payment on our future," he said hopefully. "What about that?"

She liked the futon so much better than Kitty's seduction sofa.... "No good," she said firmly, bending to heft one end. If she gave Jared an inch—or a futon—he'd take a mile. And her heart already wore his cross-trainer treads.

THREE DAYS LATER, Claire walked home from Game Night—they'd held it on Tuesday because Barry and Emily had a Valentine's Day date on Wednesday. It was a perfect February night—not quite chilly. Central Avenue was subdued and the air was filled with the scent of early citrus blossoms—like lilac and gardenia combined—but Claire's thoughts were far away....

...In Reno, where, at this moment, Jared was telling Lindi-with-an-i that he wanted a divorce. Supposedly. Then tomorrow, he would fly here and transform Valentine's Day from her suckiest holiday to the most romantic one. In theory. Jared was turning around his entire life just to be with her.

Except he'd sounded kinda faint the last time they'd talked. The Chickateers hadn't been hopeful, either. *He'll weasel out,* Emily had said, *but you stick to your guns.* Kitty kept talking about Rex's friend Dave—*he'll make you forget Jared...and your own name.*

And Zoe advised her to listen to her heart, of course. Zoe's boyfriend Brad was insisting she learn to rock climb, which she was scared to do. Kitty had decided to go with her to the class to make sure "Indiana Brad"—Kitty's new nickname for the guy—didn't push Zoe too far.

Now, as Claire approached her corner, her attention

was drawn by the sound of bluesy chords on the breeze. She squinted and made out someone sitting on the wide stone banister on her building's stairs. She got closer and saw that it was Guitar Guy. Her heart thudded in her chest. The streetlight spilled over him, dramatic and bold, sending a romantic shadow from his long body.

She realized she was walking faster.

Guitar Guy looked up, saw her and smiled. "You figure it out?" he asked, still playing.

"What? My wardrobe?" She wore a tailored white blouse with a black denim skirt. Until she could afford serious career clothes, she was at least sticking with conservative colors.

He shook his head, holding her gaze. "Whatever's been bothering you." His guitar work became a soundtrack, making it feel natural to chitchat with a stranger in the night.

"More or less." *Of course not.* She had no idea what to do about Jared. But she wasn't about to let on to Guitar Guy...who was very cute, especially with his hair cut. Kind of a young George Clooney. Dark and brooding with the kind of secret half smile that made you want to be the only one who could coax it into a full one. The streetlight gave his skin a coppery glow and his teeth seemed very white.

She wondered if he talked to all the people who came out of the building or if it was just women...or just her. "I'm Claire," she said finally.

"Nice to meet you."

"And you are...?" *Don't make me work so hard.*

"Trip."

"Excuse me?" She'd had a little wine, but she wasn't unsteady, for God's sake.

"That's my name. Trip."

"Oh," she laughed. "That's unusual. Because you like to travel?" She hoped it wasn't because of some drug thing.

"In a way."

Evasive. Maybe it *was* a drug thing. "You play very well."

"Thanks."

"Do you live around here?"

"For now. In a guest house a couple miles away."

He wasn't homeless, at least. "Guest houses are nice—cozy and efficient, with everything you need in a small space and at a small price." *Stop babbling, you dolt.* But she couldn't. Conversational gaps were like a broken filling to her. She couldn't leave them alone. "That is one great haircut," she said to keep things moving.

His gaze locked on, silver and strong, looking right into her. "And you look nice without your uniform."

"Thanks." A blush washed over her. His words and the warmth in his expression had pulled a blanket of intimacy around them on this very public corner on this major city street.

"My pleasure."

His pleasure. A blade of desire cut through her like a Ginsu knife. Wow. She was flirting with a street musician. And it was good.

Real good.

"Well, nice talking to you," he said, gently telling her goodbye. But they'd barely started.

"Yeah. You, too," she said, unable to move her feet for a few long seconds. But that was uncool, so she forced herself up the wide stairs.

"You already know the answer."

She wasn't quite sure the voice hadn't been inside

her head, so she turned and looked down at Trip. The light made him seem ghostly as a dream. "The answer?"

"To the question you're asking yourself."

It was just a throwaway line, but it shot through her like a flare, illuminating her fuzzy thinking, and she felt...better. Calm and almost confident about the Jared situation. Or maybe about something else entirely.... "I hope you're right," she said, and headed upstairs, his music wrapping around her like a caress.

From her apartment, Claire looked out her window for Trip, but he was gone. Completely. No tall shape strolling away or in the distance. Nothing. Not even a shadow. It was as if she'd just imagined him. Her confident feeling wisped away like smoke on a breeze.

THE NEXT DAY, Claire used her lunch hour to spend too much money on a black-lace teddy, a red silk sheath and a bottle of champagne. She was thinking positive about tonight with Jared, though doubts stabbed her.

Her shopping trip meant she hadn't been able to join Mimi and Georgia for lunch with Kyle Carson, an accountant who worked on the books of a company on the same floor as B&V. He was also one of Mimi's neighbors, and whenever he was in the office he would drive the three of them someplace for a nice lunch.

Kyle was good-looking and friendly and kind, and Mimi and Georgia liked to shock him with outrageous tales of their nightlife. Kyle had a live-in girlfriend, though he rarely talked about her. He'd seemed quite disappointed when Claire had said she was busy.

At the end of the day, she grabbed her shopping bag of sex appeal, removed the champagne from the B&V fridge and took the bus home.

Inside her apartment, she was startled to find Rex, Kitty's bodybuilder beau, stretched out on the sofa in black bikini underwear, looking like a model for a Campus Hotties calendar, with one of Jared's wilted roses between his teeth.

"Oh. It's you," he said around the rose stem, then took it out. Shriveled petals fell to the floor. "I thought you were Kitty."

"Sorry. Just me," she said.

"No prob." He didn't move, except to twirl the rose stem between his thumb and forefinger. More petals dropped. She slid her gaze away from the bulge in his undies and noticed her Waterford candy dish in pieces on the cocktail table.

"Had a little collision with that bowl," Rex said. "Sorry."

"It's okay," she said on a sigh. She'd known having Kitty as a roommate wouldn't be a cakewalk, but she hadn't expected to suffer glassware losses or be favored by male centerfold shots.

She headed to her room to shower and change into her teddy and red dress, and by the time she emerged, Kitty and Rex had taken off. Claire checked her watch. Jared would be landing at Sky Harbor right about now. She turned on some mood music, lit candles and sat down to wait.

And wait.

When he was an hour late, she called his cell number. Voice mail. "Just me, Jared. Was your flight delayed?"

She turned on an old *I Love Lucy* episode and heated up some of Kitty's chicken almandine leftovers. After a second madcap episode, she cracked the champagne and called again. "Where the hell are you?"

Two glasses of champagne and one blotch of paté on the carpet later, she said, "You bastard. You're not fit to...wash my windows." That was lame, but she couldn't think of the right insult—nothing too vulgar or emotionally revealing.

At ten o'clock, the phone rang. The person on the line struggled for breath. Perfect. An obscene phone call. She was about to hang up, when the voice whispered, "I couldn't do it, Claire. I'm so sorry." Jared.

"What happened?" she asked, knowing she'd hate the answer.

"Lindi's pregnant."

"She's *what*?" That was the last thing she'd expected.

"And she's so excited that I couldn't wreck it."

"Oh." Claire squeezed her eyes shut. She felt angry and bereft and...skeptical. Was Lindi-with-an-i faking? If she was wily enough to pretend to be pregnant, Claire didn't even want to mess with that. That was *Days of Our Lives* material for sure. And if Jared's wife had gotten pregnant exactly when Jared had fallen in love with Claire, she didn't need Zoe to point out the cosmic coincidence of it all.

"Well, congratulations," she said. "You'll have to forgive me if I don't rush out to buy you a cigar."

"But it's you I love, Claire. Remember that."

Yeah, right. A single tear went splat in the middle of her lap—a Rorschach blot that seemed to resemble her heart. But she wouldn't waste one more tear stain on her silk dress over this.

"And I want you," he said more urgently. "Can't we work something out?"

Here it came. *This doesn't have to change anything. I'll*

tell her. I promise. After the baby's born. Or when he's two. Make that five. Or in college.

Immediately, the Chickateers came into her mind. She imagined them sitting on the arm of the couch, legs dangling—Kitty fierce, Emily stern, Zoe worried—and they gave her the courage to say what she knew she had to.

"No way, Jared," she said, the words ringing clear as a bell. "We are so over. Don't call me again." Picturing the Chickateers high-fiving her, she dropped the phone into its cradle.

Then her heart began to ache. And throb. And burn. She had to do something to feel better. Her first thought was ice cream. If ever Claire had earned the right to eat ChocoCherry Rumba Swirl after ten, this was it. She deserved something rich and luscious and comforting. Especially because the champagne seemed to have turned her into the Leaning Tower of Claire.

In the kitchen, she spotted the champagne bottle she'd nearly emptied resting beside Jared's stupid-ass roses, droopy, dark and shriveled after a week of careful watering. She dumped the bubbly in the sink and, oblivious to the bite of thorns, tossed the roses into the trash. Valentine's Day was *so* over.

She threw open the freezer. The pint of ChocoCherry she'd bought two days ago felt suspiciously light. Inside, a frosty spoon rested on just a scrape of pink and chocolate at the bottom. *Damn it, Kitty. Tell me these things.*

If she expected to get her fat-and-sugar fix tonight, she'd have to go to the all-night grocery, where a pack of gum cost as much as the GNP of a small nation. But this was an emergency. She grabbed her purse and managed a slightly wobbly march to the elevator and then outside. She thought about what she was wearing—the sexy "getup" she'd splurged on—and her spirits sagged.

Jared's loss, she told herself, throwing back her shoulders and wavering fiercely onward in her spike heels. She deserved better than that putz, just like Georgia had said.

The evening, as lovely as the previous one, was a depressing contrast to her mood. Conversation and music leaked from the restaurants and bars she passed. At least somebody was enjoying Valentine's Day.

She read the painted window of a flower shop. "Say it with flowers. Nine-ninety-nine." Jared had said it with flowers, all right. And each bright red blossom had been a big fat lie.

So, okay, what was one more Valentine's Day as a freewheeling single woman in the city? At least she wouldn't have to face it again for three-hundred-sixty-four more days. A car slowed as it passed and two guys made disgusting tongue-licking gestures out the window at her. So romantic.

Another block and she was at Leonard's Market. She nodded at the clerk, went straight to the back and opened the door to the freezer section. Humid air billowed out, a cold caress on her skin, and she searched the frigid interior for her treasure. But there was no ChocoCherry Rumba Swirl. Damn, damn, double damn. She settled for a pint of generic mint chocolate chip and two Chipwiches—just in case—and took a balled-up twenty from her purse.

As she turned for the door, the clerk called to her, "Hope you enjoy that." He sounded so sympathetic. Could he tell she was a Valentine's Day loser? Did it show on her face? She checked herself in the fish-eye mirror over the exit door and saw half circles of mascara under each eye, with a tear trail lined in black. Pagliacci without the ruffles. She licked a finger and was scrubbing under one eye as she pushed out the door, when she thumped into something warm and human.

"Whoa!" came a male voice, rich as whiskey.

She looked up and saw Guitar Guy—Trip, she knew from the night before. "Oh, sorry. Hello," she said. This was the second time she'd crashed into him. With one mascara-decorated cheek, she probably looked like she'd covered one eye during a water pistol fight.

"Hello, yourself," he said, a light smile curving his lips. He wore a black T-shirt, a leather choker with a turquoise bead at his collarbone and comfortable-looking jeans. "Munchies?" He indicated the bag she held.

"Yeah," she said, preferring he think she was stoned instead of heartbroken.

"The munchies keep these little mom-and-pop stores alive," he said, still standing in front of her.

"I guess so," she said, dying to scrub away the remaining mascara, but not with Trip holding her gaze so intently. She stepped to the side for some room to breathe—which she realized she wasn't doing enough of.

Trip leaned to peer into her sack, his hair flopping forward. She smelled patchouli and Irish Spring. "Not bad," he said. "My personal favorite is ChocoCherry Rumba Swirl."

"Oh, mine, too. But they were out."

"It's never in stock long. Very popular flavor."

"So you shop here a lot?"

"I like to support small businesses...skip the corporate giants."

"That's nice," she said. This was so surreal. Here she was standing on Central Avenue, tipsy and weepy, wearing come-get-me pumps and a flimsy dress, discussing ice-cream favorites and corporate greed with a street musician.

And she had no intention of leaving any time soon.

"I really wanted ChocoCherry," Claire said wistfully.

"You can't always get what you want." He sang the title to the Rolling Stones song, his voice easy and beautiful.

Claire spoke the next line—about how if you tried, you sometimes got what you needed instead of what you wanted.

"Very good," he said.

"Except you have to know what you need," she said, her voice quavering a little. God, was she going to cry in front of this stranger? A handsome, sympathetic stranger, but a stranger all the same.

"You headed home?" he asked abruptly.

She nodded.

"Give me a sec and I'll walk with you."

Trip went into Leonard's and Claire remained on the sidewalk. She looked up at the silver moon, which seemed to be wearing a belligerent expression that matched her mood—*You lookin' at me?* or *You got a problem with that?*

Looking up made her dizzy and she realized the champagne was still affecting her. She was so numb, she could barely feel how cold the ice cream was against her chest. Why was she waiting for Trip? In her condition, she might say or do something crazy. Leaving would be rude. Yeah, right! That way of thinking was what got women murdered—they didn't want to hurt the serial killer's feelings.

But Trip was not dangerous. She could feel that. And when he emerged from the brightly lit store with a sack and a steaming cup of coffee, she was glad she'd waited for him. Just in time, she remembered her smeared mascara and rubbed so hard under her eye she probably took off skin.

"Something in your eye?" he asked.

"Oh, no. Kind of. Never mind." She accepted the cup he handed her. "You didn't need to get me anything," she said, but she took a sip and it was lovely and warm all the way to her tummy. At least she could feel something. "Mmm," she said.

"Oh, one more thing." He whipped a white plastic spoon out of his back pocket and handed it to her. "Dig in."

When she didn't immediately take action, he tucked his own sack under his arm so he could rummage in hers. When he lifted out the carton, the back of his hand nudged her breasts—it was an innocent gesture, but she liked it. A lot. Trip pried off the lid and tilted the ice cream at her. "Go for it. Delayed gratification isn't."

"Isn't what?" She smiled into his compassionate eyes.

"Isn't gratification. Immediate is the only gratification that counts. The behaviorists spoiled pleasure—made it too mechanistic."

What the hell was he talking about? She didn't care because he looked so handsome and kind saying it.

"Just eat," he said, chuckling. He gripped her hand around the spoon handle and dipped it into the ice cream carton. His fingers felt nice around hers—long and strong and so warm. She felt *that* all right—all the way to her toes and back up to lock on target at her sex, which pinged approvingly.

Once her spoon was heaping with green ice cream, Trip released her hand.

She brought the spoon to her mouth, watching him, then realized how bizarre this was and stopped. "Trip what?" She could not let a strange man serve her ice cream without knowing his last name. "And what do you do?" *Why are you here? Where are you going? Do you have any dangerous habits? Diseases? Can I interview your parents and your last three girlfriends?*

He chuckled softly. "Trip Osborn is my name. I play guitar, but you know that. And I guess you could say I'm a student."

"A student? Oh." She swallowed the spoonful of creamy sweetness. "Graduate school?" she asked hopefully.

"Not exactly. I audit a couple of classes with a visiting philosophy professor. Shall we walk?" he said, gesturing with the ice-cream carton.

Claire nodded, took another swallow of coffee—a lovely contrast to the icy treat—and they set off, walking companionably close. Trip was taller than Claire and not broad, but he had presence. He felt very there, very solid. She reached to scoop more ice cream out of the carton he held, which made him stop walking. She realized she was being selfish, drinking coffee and eating the ice cream all alone.

"Want some?" She held out her spoon. Odd to share utensils with a stranger, but what else could she do?

"Great idea." He whipped another plastic spoon from his jeans, like a magician tugging a scarf from a secret pocket, then scooped out a bite, the muscles in his hand and forearm rippling. His skin had a thick velvety look, as if the tissue itself were muscular. She felt another internal ping.

"Mmm," he said, savoring the ice cream. His rumbly musician's voice made the sound completely sexual. More pinging.

Claire knew her tipsiness was making her overreact, so she focused on finding out more about him. "So, you're majoring in philosophy?"

He chuckled again. "No more than anyone, I guess. Isn't that our job as humans, to figure out what life means to us, what we believe it's all about?"

"I guess so," she said and hiccupped, which threw her off balance and she sort of stumbled in her heels.

"Hey, there," he said, propping her back on her feet, the little gesture making him seem solid and protective. He looked down at her feet. "How do you balance on those things?"

She wore yet another pair of uncomfortable shoes, chosen this time for their sex appeal. "God only knows," she said and with a laugh she kicked them off, watching as they shot down the sidewalk in front of them, one after the other.

"Better?" he asked.

"Much," she said. The concrete felt cool and solid against her soles. She felt planted on the ground, not teetering over it. Even the grit felt good. She sure didn't care about her Hanes-Her-Way stockings. Her evening was in shreds, so why shouldn't her panty hose be, too?

They walked toward her shoes. In the spirit of the moment, she had the urge to just leave them—Cinderella drop-kicking her glass slippers. *Screw you, Prince Charming. And you can keep the shoes.*

But Trip collected them, one after the other, slipping them into his sack. What had he bought at Leonard's anyway? He made her so curious. Where did he come from? Did he like her? *No, no. That was dumb.* He probably bought coffee for all the women who bumped into him in short red dresses and stilettos.

She swallowed more coffee and took another bite of ice cream to stabilize her wild thoughts. "Now that you mention it, I kind of get paid for my philosophy," she said.

"How's that?"

"I work for an advertising agency. We try to shape attitudes and beliefs. Capitalize on them."

"Ah, perpetuating consumerism—cashing in on the myth that more is better and you can buy love, security and happiness?"

"Pretty much," she said, getting a twinge from his disapproval, but not much bothered by it.

"It's a new job, though," he said.

"What makes you think that?"

"The way you look in the mornings—a little uncertain."

That irritated her, though she was flattered that he'd paid that much attention. "What you've seen is me in a hurry. Though I have changed my approach to work, I guess."

"How so?"

"I've been working harder. Being more deliberate about it."

"Why?"

"To make progress."

"Toward what?"

"More responsibility. More respect. More money, I guess."

"How about more joy? More satisfaction?"

"So, this is why you're a philosophy major? So you can give people grief about their lives?"

"Oh, absolutely." He grinned and dug into the ice cream, his wrist turning, muscles rippling.

"And, sure, I'll have more satisfaction," she said. "Doing well is always satisfying."

He looked at her as if that weren't necessarily so.

"What else do you do?" she asked. "Besides play guitar and criticize people's world view?"

"You mean for a living?" He bit the ice cream off his spoon. "This and that. I make enough to do what I want."

"You're a good guitarist. Are you in a band?"

"I sit in with people when I feel like it or they need me. Nothing permanent." He stopped so she could spoon out more ice cream. "I don't do permanent," he said, as if in answer to a question she hadn't asked.

"How long have you been in Phoenix?"

"Not long."

"How long will you stay?"

"Long enough," he said, looking straight into her eyes. Because of her? Is that what he meant? Heat cascaded down her body, scalp to toe, in a warm bath of pleasure.

This was insane, of course. Gushing and blushing over a little flirtation with a near stranger. Heartbreak and champagne did funny things to you.

Things she liked. They kept walking and talking and eating ice cream. Trip told her about the retired blues guitarist he took lessons from, about his philosophy class and about people he'd met playing right on her corner. She told him a little about her work and the agency, swept away by laughter and pleasure and sparks. She felt clever and wry and smart-assed—not at all weak and weepy and heartbroken.

Now and then she leaned against him to make a remark, behaving like Kitty—flirtatious and fun. And she loved every minute of it.

Before she knew it they'd reached the wide front steps of CityScapes and she had to go in. She looked up at the building. Jared's betrayal had taken away some of the joy she felt about the place.

She sighed, then turned to Trip, sorry to say goodnight. "Thanks for walking with me."

His eyes warmed with compassion. "One more thing to cheer you up." He reached into his sack and brought out a foil-wrapped chocolate Santa as big as a salad plate stuck on a stick. "Merry Christmas," he said.

Claire accepted the gift, her mouth open in surprise.

"Since Valentine's Day hasn't been good to you, I backed up a holiday. Might be a bit stale."

She laughed.

"Valentine's Day is a racket built on guilt and duty, Claire."

"You sound like my roommate Kitty. She says it's a conspiracy of the jewelry industry."

"I like how she thinks," he said. "Love doesn't care about the calendar."

"Damn straight. Love has no *sell by* date," she added, trying to be more flip than she felt.

"Now you're getting it."

"This was kind of you." She held up the Santa and twirled it. The red foil caught the light like sparks.

Trip shrugged, leaned slightly away, his eye on the sidewalk ahead, where he seemed to want to go.

"So, you live nearby?" she asked, holding him with her words.

"For now. The owner wants to sell the place, though."

"You'll have to move?"

He nodded.

"Doesn't that bother you? Not knowing where you'll go or where you'll live?"

"Not really. Security is an illusion. This way I appreciate every moment."

That could sound like such a line, but from Trip it seemed sincere and profound. Maybe it was his voice—the warm, low rasp of it, melodic but restrained, like he was holding back its richness so it wouldn't overwhelm her.

"Interesting point of view," she said.

"Nothing's really permanent."

"I'll say." She meant Jared and their false happiness.

"Not even the bad stuff," he added softly, his gaze digging in, willing her to believe him. "Whoever he is, he lost out."

Wow. Silence beat between them. It was there again, that intimate blanket Trip managed to pull around them so that Claire felt close to him, as if he could read her mind, sense her hurt and understood it all.

"He turned out to be married," she said, relieved to say it out loud. "He was supposed to tell his wife about us and fly here tonight, but his wife is pregnant—or so she says—so he couldn't leave her."

"That's hard news."

"Yeah."

"And this was for him?" he said, looking her up and down, a flare of heat in his eyes.

She nodded, feeling stupid in the sexy outfit. "I'm an idiot, right?"

"No. You're a romantic. And you look great."

"Thanks. You're sure making me feel better." She raised the foil-covered Santa as proof.

"I couldn't let an emotion-exploitive holiday ruin things, could I?" He kept looking at her face, making her uncomfortable and overheated. When had he moved so close? Close enough that he could kiss her...and see every fleck of mascara under her eye.

She stepped back and turned slightly away. "I'm a mess."

"Uh-uh." Trip took her by the upper arms and made her look at him. "You're beautiful." Then he focused on the right side of her face. "Except for a little something here...."

She thought he meant the mascara, but he touched her cheekbone, then licked his finger. "Mmm. Chocolate mint."

"Yeah?" She could still feel the pressure of his fingertip on her skin.

"Yeah." It was so quiet and Trip's expression was so intimate and he was so close...and moving closer, leaning in. Lord, he was going to kiss her. And she was going to like it.

A lot.

"Is that all of it?" she whispered, encouraging him.

"There might be a little more—" he leaned in "—right—" moved closer, tilted his mouth "—here." And then he kissed her—his lips warm and giving, a flesh pillow on which her mouth could rest. For a long time.

Oh, yes. Yes, yes. The kiss tasted cool and hot and of mint and chocolate and it was full of promise and held-back need. Maybe it was because of her heartbreak, or the champagne, or Valentine's Day, or the chocolate Santa, or Trip's skill, or all of them combined, but this was the most romantic kiss she'd ever shared.

After a long, glorious moment, Trip broke away.

"You sure you got it all?" she mumbled, leaning in, dazed.

He chuckled. "Unfortunately, yeah. I'm sure."

She blew out a breath. "Wow."

"Yeah, wow. You'd better go up," he said, handing her the nearly empty ice-cream carton. "Before I go after your Santa." *And you.* That was what he meant and a chill raced through her. He backed away smiling.

She turned and scurried upward, the chocolate Santa clutched in her hand, her heart pounding, full of feeling.

Inside her apartment, she shut the door and rested her back against it. What had just happened? She'd kissed a stranger and loved it. Not quite a stranger. She knew his name and what kind of ice cream he liked, right? She touched her lips, which still tingled.

She looked down at her feet, bare inside her panty hose. Trip still had her shoes! Now she knew how Cinderella must have felt after her night at the ball—excited and dreamy and full of hope about miracles and magic. Claire checked the clock. Midnight. Cinderella's deadline.

She had it better than Cinderella, though. Her Prince Charming knew exactly where to bring back her glass slippers. She couldn't wait to see him again.

Then the phone rang. She listened until the machine picked up and heard Jared, his voice plaintive and sad, swearing his undying love, promising they could work it out, begging for another chance.

Her euphoria faded and she braced for the return of her heartbreak. Except nothing happened. She felt no agony. No all-body toothache. What the hell? Somehow, her hurt over Jared had been cauterized by her ice-cream chat with Trip.

Thoughtfully, she peeled the foil from the candy Santa and nibbled carefully at the top of his cap. She had the uneasy feeling that what she'd *thought* she felt for Jared had been what she thought she *should* feel. Maybe she'd just been in love with love....

That idea was way too hard to follow on three-fourths of a bottle of champagne. It was a brain twister and her brain had gone through enough contortions for one night.

All she knew for sure was that, despite everything, she'd had a wonderful Valentine's Day. Romantic and tender and surprising and sweet. That was what she'd remember. Period.

Throwing caution to the wind, Claire snapped off Santa's chocolate head with one quick bite.

4

THE NEXT MORNING, Claire woke to sunlight burning holes in her hungover eyes and a mouth parched and bitter from too much champagne and ice cream, not to mention the chocolate Santa she'd beheaded.

The memory of Trip's kiss came into her mind, delicious and melty, and for a second it cured her hangover. Then her thoughts moved to Jared and his pregnant wife, but that was no fun, so she shifted back to Trip and his mouth, his gray see-all eyes. Mmmm. She felt warm all over.

Maybe it was too soon, maybe she was just hiding from her heartbreak, but thinking about Trip made her feel better and that was enough for now.

She chose an A-line jean skirt, which she dressed up with a pink cotton blouse with three-quarter sleeves, buttoning the top fake-pearl button so she'd look more serious. She wondered what Trip would say about her "getup." He'd probably be waiting for her on the corner with her shoes...and maybe another kiss.

That made her smile big, which made her scalp ache and her eyes burn. She was never, never, never drinking champagne again.

In the kitchen, she poured coffee beans into Kitty's grinder and pushed the button. The buzz cut through her skull like a chainsaw.

"Keep it down!" came Kitty's muffled shout.

No kidding. Claire grabbed her throbbing head. "Sorry!" Kitty must have come back from Rex's some time in the night. Claire would tell her about the Jared mess, but not about Trip and the kiss. Too bizarre. Too crazy. Too wonderful.

She could still feel the frisson of electricity between their lips and Trip's broad, warm hand at her waist, holding her softly, but with the promise of strength and desire.

The coffee made her stomach burn, so she snatched a liquid yogurt drink from the fridge and decided to head for work early.

She rushed out of the lobby and down the stairs, where she faced forward and kept her smile relaxed, so she wouldn't seem too eager. The possibility that Trip waited for her outside made her overworked heart lurch into high gear. *Again with the adrenaline?* she could almost hear it say. She concentrated on her peripheral vision and listened for a guitar.

Silence. And no one around. Her heart slowed to a dull, sad rhythm. Oh, well. Maybe after work.

"Claire?"

She turned, hoping for Trip, but got Mitch the doorman.

"You flew by so fast I couldn't catch you. A guy left this." He handed her a paper sack.

Inside were Claire's shoes. Trip had dropped them off, not even waiting to talk to her. Prince Charming had done his good deed and it was over. No promise of eternal love or offer of the kingdom, just her scuffed and dusty heels. She fought her disappointment.

It made sense, really. He'd felt sorry for the tipsy, tear-streaked, wobbly woman who'd thumped into him at Leonard's. The comforting walk and the chocolate Santa were a pity package, with the kiss as the bow on top. She knew better than to trust her instincts.

Except there was something else in the sack. Something wrapped in green paper, which turned out to be a small bouquet of yellow flowers with large brown centers—brown-eyed Susans, she thought they were called.

All the way to the office, she wondered what they meant. More sympathy? A thank-you? An invitation? What?

She entered Biggs & Vega, the shoe sack under her arm, the bouquet in one hand, feeling woozy and very hungover.

"You shouldn't have," Georgia said from the receptionist desk, nodding at the flowers. "Though I'd love you to pick up my dry cleaning."

"Maybe after you give me that neck massage you keep promising."

"One of these days." Georgia scrutinized her. "You look rode hard and put away wet, girl. You *earn* those posies last night?"

"I had a little too much champagne, that's all."

"There's V-8 in the fridge and tabasco in the cupboard. And if you don't mind a furtive nipple rub, I think Leroy the Letch has some vodka in his file cabinet. Hair of the dog?"

"I'll be fine, but thanks," Claire said, and headed to her office, her stomach roiling unhappily. She had a strategy meeting with Ryan in a half hour and she had to be perky enough to evade any octopus action. She'd check e-mail, then take a cat nap at her desk.

She was pleased to find a message from Arthur Biggs announcing a pro bono promotion for New View House Rehab, the favorite charity of B&V's biggest client, Arthur Greystone, who had asked B&V to donate an ad campaign to increase contributions to the place. In the e-mail, Biggs assigned the project to Ryan Ames, her mentor.

What a coup! Ryan always complained about extra work. She could offer to help and if he'd let her take the lead, she could show her stuff on the project. Those things were always high visibility. She printed out the e-mail for their meeting, then rested her weary head on her desk for a quick snooze....

"Are you okay?" Ryan's voice made her start and she jerked up, then grabbed her head, which hadn't appreciated the move.

"I'm fine," she said.

Ryan had dropped to his haunches beside her desk, at eye level. "You don't look very fine." He patted her forearm, then left his hand there. "Want to tell your mentor all about it?" He tilted his face at a too-friendly angle. Blech.

"Really, I'm okay," she said, pushing her chair a couple of feet away. The movement jiggled her already-shaky stomach, which gave her an idea that would probably take care of Ryan's amorous impulses. "I mean, I *will* be okay...as soon as I throw up my guts."

Ryan blanched, then pushed to his feet. "Oh. Gee. Sorry."

"I'll just head to the ladies' room," she said, standing. "How about I meet you in your office in ten minutes?"

He held the door for her. "We can reschedule if you're not feeling well...."

"No, no. The show must go on. Just one quick upchuck and I'll be good as new." The look on his face was priceless.

After a quick splash of water to perk herself up, Claire headed to Ryan's office, quite pleased with her stunt—even more so when he kept his distance all through the meeting. Maybe she'd turn this into an on-going condition—something contagious.

She'd also been right that Ryan wasn't pleased with the extra project and was happy to have her help. They'd work *closely*, he'd said, winking. *Maybe meet over dinners.*

What a horn dog. If it came to that, she'd borrow Emily's neighbor's kids and meet Ryan at the nearest kiddie-filled Chuck E. Cheese. She'd handle Ryan, all right, if it meant progress on her career. Before they ended the meeting, Ryan e-mailed Arthur Biggs about inviting Claire onto the campaign. All she needed now was Biggs's okay.

Back at her office, Claire kept getting distracted by the bouquet of brown-eyed Susans Trip had given her. She'd set them in a plastic tumbler on the corner of her desk beside the sack of shoes...a little reminder of her ice-cream stroll with Prince Charming, the memory of which clung to her like a dream.

She lifted the flowers from the water-filled cup and buried her nose in the blossoms, letting the petals tickle her cheeks and upper lip. She took a deep inhalation of the fresh scent. A petal shot up her nose. She tried to sniff it out, but it seemed to be stuck.

It tickled and itched, torturing her nasal passage. Maybe she was allergic, too, because her eyes burned like hell. She sneezed. Still there. She dropped the flowers and pressed one nostril closed, then took a deep breath, ready to snort the thing out...except just then Arthur Biggs appeared in her doorway.

Oh, God. Claire pretended to be rubbing her nose. "Come on in," she said.

Biggs approached her desk.

She leaned over to put the daisies back, but knocked the plastic tumbler forward, sending a wave of water onto Biggs's undoubtedly hand-tailored slacks.

"Whoa!" he said, jumping back.

"Sorry, sorry." She lunged over the desk to grab the cup, giving Biggs, who'd bent to pick up the flowers, a tremendous peek down her blouse, she realized too late. She retreated to her chair.

Biggs put the flowers back in the cup, then brushed at his pants.

"I'll get those cleaned for you," she said, remembering with chagrin that barely two months ago she'd spilled red punch on the man's shoes. She was not generally clumsy. Only when her career hung in the balance. Sheesh.

"It's fine," he said. "No problem." Maybe he didn't remember about the punch.

"How can I help you, Mr. Biggs...um, Arthur?" They were peers, she reminded herself, even though he was old enough to be her father, so she should use his first name. Her nose itched like mad. Her eyes watered viciously.

"Ames tells me he wants you on the New View House project."

"Oh, yes. I'm very excited about that." She twitched her nose, trying to dislodge the petal or get it into a less annoying crevice.

"That's good," he said, giving her an odd look. He

rubbed his upper lip. Did he doubt her? Think she was a ditz? Maybe he did remember about the punch.

"I'll give it my best," she said, trying to sound professional while twitching her nose like a spastic bunny.

"Ames vouches for you," he said, but he wouldn't quite meet her gaze. "The halfway house is Winston Greystone's baby and he'll want a bigger campaign than we can afford. We need you to control costs but keep him happy."

"We'll be completely frugal. And absolutely diplomatic."

"Greystone Properties is very important to us, so kid gloves and ego strokes."

"Absolutely." God, her nose was killing her. If only he would leave so she could hit the restroom and clear the flora from her sinuses. This was her chance to impress Biggs, but all she wanted was a tissue and a honk.

"I'll want you to meet Winston, of course. He'll be at the party. You'll be there, right?"

"Of course." The B&V annual party was a don't-miss company event that included employees and major clients and everyone's spouse or significant other. Lots of boozing, schmoozing and ass-kissing. She had planned to bring Jared because a boyfriend would make her seem more mature and responsible. But now she'd be going alone. "I'm sure we'll have the campaign in good shape by then," she said.

"Great. Good to hear," he said, rubbing his upper lip thoughtfully. "I like to see our young staffers so go-go."

"Thank you. I'm as go-go as I can possibly be-be." What an idiot.

Biggs smiled at her weak joke, then turned to go, brushing at his wet crotch as he walked away.

The instant he turned the corner, Claire barreled into the bathroom where the mirror revealed that in addition to the daisy petal up her nose, there were two plastered to her upper lip like mustachios. No wonder Biggs kept rubbing his lip. Like when a friend had spinach between her teeth and you licked yours as an unconscious hint.

With all the twitching she'd done, the man probably thought snorting flower petals was some new drug thing. *As go-go as I can possibly be-be.* She cringed. That was as dumb-dumb as she could possibly get-get. Plus, she'd made him look like he'd wet his pants. So much for good impressions. She gently thumped her forehead against the cool tile wall a couple of times— which did not help her hangover one bit.

The good news was that at least his odd expression had been due to her petal moustache, not his doubts about her skills. And he'd sounded honestly pleased she'd be working on the campaign—and about her enthusiasm.

She reached her office and found Kyle Carson waiting for her. "Have you had lunch yet?" he asked.

"No, actually. And I'm thinking of skipping it. Killer hangover."

"How about soup? The vichyssoise at Vito's Bistro would be perfect for coating your stomach. It'd be nice and soothing."

Kyle was such a thoughtful guy. "I guess so," Claire said. "If that's where Mimi and Georgia want to go."

"It's just you and me today." Kyle cleared his throat. Huh? What was this about? She was curious, but not uncomfortable. Kyle was no Ryan Ames. He wouldn't cheat on his girlfriend. Claire went to get her purse.

Five minutes later, Kyle held the passenger door of his excruciatingly neat Audi sedan as she slid in. He came around, hung his suit jacket on a hanger in the back seat beside his briefcase, which rested squarely in place. So fussy for a straight guy.

At the restaurant, the hostess took them to a booth, where Ryan ordered her chamomile tea to settle her stomach. So sweet. Now Kyle was the kind of guy she should be dating—honest, mature, stable. Cute, too. But he was taken. The good ones always were. She hoped his girlfriend appreciated what she had.

"So, how about going out with me?" Kyle blurted. "I was thinking skiing a week from Saturday?" He stared at her and swallowed nervously.

"You want me to go out with you? Skiing?" Was this cheating thing spreading like a virus? "I don't ski, actually...." She stared at him. "What about your girlfriend, Kyle?"

Color shot up his cheeks from his neck. "We, uh, broke up," he said. "I thought you knew."

"No, I didn't. I'm sorry."

"Don't be. It's been a month. Long enough that I should be ready to move on." He shrugged. "Mimi told me you just split with your boyfriend, too, so I thought we could, um, get together."

Thank you, Mimi. What a great idea. Kyle didn't give her a zing, but then she'd just broken up with Jared, so her zinger was still numb, right? And the Trip zing? Champagne-induced, of course.

"So, I thought going up to Flagstaff to ski would be something different...but if you don't ski..." He flushed, as if uncertain what to say next.

"We could do something else," she said, rushing to ease his nervousness. "Anything you want. Whatever you enjoy."

"Oh. Well, I, uh, do have season tickets to the symphony. I was going to sell next week's tickets to someone, but since you don't ski, we might as well use them. They're paid for and all."

Touched by his jitters, she said, "The symphony would be lovely." The symphony? Hello? The symphony was for blue hairs who toddled over after the early-bird prime rib special at Beefeaters. It was *mature*, though. And adult. And didn't she want a mature, adult life?

"Great," Kyle said, blowing out a breath. "It's a date."

Claire was pretty darn pleased with herself. She hadn't yet dipped a spoon into her vichyssoise and she had a date with an appropriate man. This was exactly what she needed. The encounter with Trip had helped her move on. And now she could start a sensible relationship with Kyle. This could be perfect.

TRIP WATCHED THE BUS lumber away from Claire's corner and checked his watch. Five-thirty. She usually came home on this bus, but she hadn't bounced off.

He'd had to rush to get here in time. He'd been looking after the landlord's kids—home early from school—so the woman could make some business calls. A single mom, she had her hands full raising two boys and running her mail-order business. The boys were boisterous and smart, and he liked hanging with them. Growing up, he'd always enjoyed the younger foster kids. He'd liked teaching them things.

That was why he'd signed up to teach at Rosie's

House, a place in South Phoenix Erik had turned him on to that provided instruments and lessons for poor kids who wouldn't otherwise be able to use their talent. Every city had ways you could help, he'd found.

Now he stared down Central. No sign of another bus. Where was Claire? And, furthermore, what the hell was he doing here? By rights, he should have taken one more run with the palm crew, even though his shoulders ached. He needed grocery money.

Sometimes the effort required to maintain the life he'd chosen wearied him—especially when he had other things on his mind. Like Claire. He just wanted to be sure she'd gotten his flowers. And that she was all right about the kiss.

Which had been a mistake. She'd been upset and tipsy and he'd gotten carried away. But the memory had stayed with him—the hitch in her breath, the way she'd tasted—cool mint and chocolate with an overlay of coffee. Like a holiday. And like her. A sweet spice that was all Claire.

But she was not the kind of woman he got involved with. She was too intense and way too serious. She had a plan and he hated plans. And even if he did stay to explore the heat between them, he didn't have what she wanted. He wasn't capable of it.

He stared up at her terrace—he'd figured which glass door was hers by watching for a light after she'd gone upstairs last night. There was no sign of life right now.

He thought of how she'd looked in that hot dress and impossible heels. All for a married jerk, who'd broken her heart. That sent a spike of anger through him. Odd. He didn't usually get that fired up about anything.

There was just so much feeling in her face. She had a sharp sense of irony, but she was so damned earnest, ready to get back in there and try, try again. He wanted to see happy emotions in her wide-open eyes, not betrayal, loneliness and hurt.

He, of course, could hurt her, too. Maybe already had by kissing her, then just leaving her the shoes and flowers. He was his own brand of jerk with women. He'd learned that from Nancy. *You're never really here, are you? You always hold back. You never really connect.* And he'd realized she was right. As much as he'd wanted to get close, he'd felt distant, removed from his emotions and from the people he cared about most.

At first, he'd thought it was because of losing his foster family, but the feeling stayed on after he left Nancy, like some chronic condition. The message was clear: Don't get too close.

So now he enjoyed women, but only if things were simple. Sex or friendship. Occasionally both, but only short-term. And sex would never be simple with Claire. That was as obvious as her smile was bright.

All the same, he would hang around to make sure she was all right, that she understood. After that, maybe he'd stay clear of her corner for a while. Until the heat faded.

CLAIRE GRABBED THE SACK with her shoes and the flowers Trip had given her and stood to go home. It was six-thirty. She'd stayed late—just like the hard-driving account execs at B&V. Well, except for that long lunch with Kyle.

She was definitely making progress. After lunch, she'd met with Ryan and the creative team—an artist and a copywriter—about the New View House campaign and things were humming along.

She paused for another sniff of the flowers, careful not to inhale too deeply. She hadn't thought about Trip more than a couple of times since she'd made her date with Kyle. And her hangover had faded altogether.

Last, she grabbed her briefcase, which now contained a folder labeled "New View House," instead of just a few pens and some paper clips. She had some work she could do at home.

A half hour later, she stepped off the bus on her corner, her mind full of ideas for New View House, raring to get started.

Then she heard music and saw Trip. She stopped dead and last night rushed back to her, brushing away her work thoughts like so much dust off a desk. He was playing something complicated for a handful of people. He looked so good, so familiar. She had felt those lips on hers, those fingers on her skin. She moved forward on legs as wobbly as noodles.

When he looked up and saw her, he grinned and hit a wrong chord. She'd flustered him. Wow. Had he come here just for her? When he cut the song short and headed her way, she thought so.

"I see you got the flowers," he said, nodding at the bouquet she carried.

"Yes. They're beautiful. And thanks for bringing back my shoes." She lifted the sack.

"Are you okay?" he asked. The compassion in his expression confirmed her fears. That had definitely been a pity kiss. Crap. If only she hadn't blurted the humiliating Jared story. "Of course. I'm fine. I was so wasted! Sorry I got obnoxious."

"You weren't obnoxious," he said, standing only

inches away. "You were funny and brave and beautiful." His eyes steadied her. "And you have great taste in ice cream."

She flushed with pleasure. "That chocolate Santa was a godsend. I worked out my aggressions snapping off his head."

"Exactly what I had in mind."

She had the insane desire to lean in and kiss him again. Just to see if last night's magic was a one-time thing. But Trip moved to sit on the cement banister and patted a spot beside him.

Claire joined him, putting her briefcase, the flowers and the sack of shoes to one side, liking the fact that their arms brushed. "Last night was fun," she said, determined to stay casual.

"For me, too." He shifted so he could look into her face. "I wanted to make sure you were all right...with what happened."

He was closing things off. He was right, of course. Heck, she had a date a week from Saturday with a responsible, serious guy with an actual job, not a street musician-slash-sort-of-student.

So, why was she nearly shivering with lust?

"I'm fine with it," she said. "Great, in fact. It was..." Amazing, inspiring, hotter than hot.

"I know what you mean," he said with a sigh that told her the kiss hadn't been *all* mercy. "But you're just getting over a guy and I'm just passing through."

"Sure. That makes sense."

"I'm glad you liked the flowers. They reminded me of you."

"Because I have brown eyes?"

"That...and they're fresh and sturdy and very alive." His gray eyes roved her face. There was more he wasn't saying and that made her heart start to pound.

But just when she thought he might say something intimate, he said, "I should take off." He surprised her by cupping her cheek. "Take care of yourself, Claire."

"But you'll be back, won't you? I mean, to play?" She could kill herself for sounding so eager.

"Hard to say." He must have read the disappointment in her eyes, because he said, "You'll see me again, Claire. I like downtown people."

She was way too glad.

BUT TRIP DIDN'T APPEAR on the corner the next day. Or the next. By the fifth day, she stopped watching for him. But, a week after their chocolate mint kiss, she was racing for the bus and there he was, playing on her corner like the day she'd crashed into him.

He nodded at her, but kept performing for the cluster of people who stood around his guitar case, not missing a note. She didn't fluster him this time. Sad. The bus roared up and it seemed stupid to miss it just to talk to him, so she bounded up the steps.

"Claire!"

She turned, delighted to hear her name on his lips, pleased by his smile.

"I'll come by after work, so we can talk," he said.

"Great," she said, ridiculously happy at the prospect.

EXCEPT CLAIRE was so late leaving work that night, she was sure he'd have gone by the time she got home. When she found him waiting for her on the stone banister, his guitar in its case, her heart rose in her throat.

He'd waited for her. She hurried to sit beside him. "I'm so sorry I'm late."

He shrugged like it was no big deal.

"Really. I didn't mean to hold you up."

"It's all good, Claire," he said, giving her leg the briefest pat. "Before you got here, I met a guy from Las Vegas who counts cards in blackjack for a living. Very cool guy. If you'd come sooner, I would have missed him."

"You seem to meet a lot of interesting people."

"Everybody's interesting if you give them a chance to tell their story. So how was your day?" His eyes reached in, pulling at her, fully focused on whatever she wanted to tell him.

She told him she was going out to New View House on Saturday to scope it out. All by herself. Ryan had a soccer game with his son and the creative team told her to just take good notes. Being sent to scout the place was proof that Ryan trusted her judgment, but she was nervous about doing a good job. When she mentioned that Ryan kept sort of hitting on her, Trip suggested a knee to the groin, which made her laugh.

Trip, in turn, told her about a writer whose palms he'd trimmed who'd just gotten a nibble on his screenplay—at age ninety—and more about Erik Terrifik.

They were engrossed in a discussion of the differences between Delta and Chicago blues—Claire hadn't a clue, but Trip made it fascinating—when the front door to CityScapes opened and they both looked up to see Kitty emerge, flanked by two muscle-bound guys—Rex and someone Claire hadn't met.

Claire jumped to her feet and moved away from Trip, embarrassed for some reason.

"It's about time you got home!" Kitty said, checking out Trip, then Claire. "We've been waiting for an hour and you left your cell phone on the charger so we couldn't call you. This is Dave," Kitty said, indicating the hulk beside Rex.

"Nice to meet you," Claire said. Dave was the guy Kitty claimed would make her forget her own name. He was good looking and large—as tall, broad and thick-limbed as a superhero.

"And who's this?" Kitty continued. She held out her hand to Trip. "I'm Claire's roommate, Kitty."

Trip smiled and shook her hand.

"This is Trip Osborn," Claire said quickly. "We were just talking." She made it sound like they'd been caught naked in a closet.

"Nice to meet you," Kitty said, raising her brows at Claire—*What's all this now?*

"Well, nice of you to say hi and I'm glad to meet you, Dave," Claire said, hoping to shoo Kitty and her body-guards off.

"Oh, but you're coming with us," Kitty said, linking arms with her. "First to the gym for a Tae-Bo class, and then dinner at Veggie Annie's."

"But I just got home," Claire said, even though she'd been sitting here long enough for her butt to go numb.

"You have to eat." Kitty yanked.

"But I'm not dressed for the gym." Claire hated exercise and nut cutlet restaurants that smelled like B vitamins and made you feel guilty for using salt. She'd much rather talk about Jelly Roll Morton or existentialism with Trip.

"I've got stuff you can borrow." Kitty patted her gym bag. "Come on. We've got fifteen minutes before the warm up."

"See you around," Trip said, standing to go. He seemed amused by the dispute.

But when? Want to meet at Leonard's? Do our laundry together? Something?

She said goodbye to Trip and let herself be swept into the back seat of Kitty's car with Dave, who filled the space with his he-man body and enough Polo cologne to sear her nose hairs.

"So, you get to know homeless guys a lot?" Dave asked her.

"He's not homeless," Claire said defensively. "He's a musician. And a graduate philosophy student." Sort of. "He lives a very stimulating life."

"Stimulating, huh?" Kitty said, turning to talk over the seat. "Dave, why don't you tell Claire about your last rugby match? Now that's what I call stimulating."

Dave talked all the way to the health club. Yawn. Then, five minutes into the Tae-Bo class, Claire got a thigh-sized Charlie horse that Dave heroically tried to rub out, leaving finger bruises on her calves. Then the three health nuts harangued Claire for eating Cheetos while she waited for the class to end.

And all through their grainy tofu salads and dry-as-dust garbanzo burgers at Veggie Annie's, Dave regaled her with stories of rugby injuries, critiqued the out-of-shape slobs he trained and outlined the merits of the home gym system he sold on the side.

He was gorgeous, though, and at a primitive level Claire responded to him. She got a ping, not zing. Evidently, the zing required more than physical appeal. She maybe could manage having sex with Dave, but he'd have to be quiet, and judging by how much he liked hearing himself talk, that wasn't likely.

Claire kept giving Kitty signals to head home, but

Kitty was indomitable, even when it was clear that Dave had given up, too. In the end, Dave and Claire played Tetris on Kitty's Palm Pilot in the back seat while Kitty and Rex made out at stoplights.

When they finally dropped Dave off in the parking lot, he promised to send Claire the home gym promotional package and guaranteed her a discount.

As soon as she got upstairs, she broke out the Chipwiches—on general principles—and checked messages. She deleted another plaintive Jared call, grateful she was past that misstep on the journey to her perfect life.

She was still uncertain about love, but she'd learned a couple things in the past two days. It had to be more than physical—Thighmaster Dave had shown her that. She needed intellectual stimulation, too. Like with Trip? He was funny and smart and interesting and different—maybe too different.

She needed someone with similar interests and a life she recognized. Someone like Kyle. Yeah. Kyle was right on target.

Still, she couldn't help wondering when she would see Trip again. And what his guest house looked like. And his bed. And his body. Naked.

Bad, bad Claire. Where was Georgia with that rolled-up newspaper when she needed a whack on the nose?

5

ON SATURDAY MORNING, Claire turned the key of Emily's Volvo, which she'd borrowed to go to New View House, and it purred powerfully to life. Great car. In fact, the night before, she'd sampled the joys of car ownership by driving out to Tempe in the Volvo to wander the shops and bars near ASU.

After the pro bono campaign, she'd get better accounts, she was certain, and a raise, so she could afford her own car. Maybe not right away and maybe nothing bigger than a wind-up toy, but something.

She had just headed for a street that would get her to the freeway when the Volvo rabbit-jumped and died. She coasted to the curb, threw the car in park and tried the key. The engine turned over and over, fighting valiantly to start, but no dice.

A tap on the passenger window made her look up. She was startled to see Trip smiling at her through the glass. She pushed the button and the window hummed down. "What are you doing here?" she asked, flummoxed by her dilemma and the sight of him.

"Music," he said, indicating the shop behind him—Ziggie's—where he must have been when he'd spotted her. "Car trouble?"

"Looks that way," she said, pumping the gas pedal fiercely, then trying again. Nothing. "I borrowed this car and...uh-oh."

Emily had told her to put gas in it, but she'd assumed she'd meant before bringing it back—Emily was kind of tight about money—but she must have meant it was low on fuel. Claire had gone all the way to Tempe and back without giving a thought to gas. What an idiot. "I think I'm out of gas," she admitted, giving the steering wheel a frustrated thump. The horn blasted. She jumped.

"Hang on. I'll get some," Trip said. Before she could object, he'd trotted off, his guitar case slung over his back by its strap. She hadn't seen him since Thursday night's encounter with Kitty and the Hurt Patrol. She'd missed him, she realized with a sigh, watching him lope down the street.

Where was he going to get gas? There wasn't a service station for miles. Cars whipped by, making the Volvo shudder. At the very least, she should go with him, not sit here like some helpless damsel in distress.

She got out of the car, but saw that Trip was already headed back with a gas can. She pulled the lever that freed the tank cap and waited for him beside her rear bumper.

"Got it from the yard guys down the block," he said, tilting the spout into the opening. "For their mowers."

Gas fumes rose between them.

"Very resourceful," she said, embarrassed by her flub. "I shouldn't have forgotten gas. I usually don't do stupid things like that. Except when I'm nervous or preoccupied or..."

"It's okay, Claire. Go give it a try." He nodded toward the front of the car, then followed her, leaning in the window to watch.

Claire held her breath and turned the key. The engine struggled, stuttered, coughed, then roared to life.

Whew! She turned to Trip, breathing in his lovely patchouli-and-soap scent. "Thanks a lot. How much do I owe you?"

"A smile. I was glad to help," he said.

"At least let me give you a ride somewhere."

He looked at her, considering. "Where are you headed?"

"To Mesa and the halfway house, but I'll take you wherever you need to go."

"How about if I come along? I don't have to be anywhere right now and it sounds interesting. If I won't be in the way."

"No, no. I'm sure you'll be fine." Who was she kidding? She was delighted to have him along, happy for the chance to spend time with him, listening to his whiskey voice and rumbling laugh, catching his mysterious smile.

He called a farewell to someone in the door of the music store, put his guitar in the back seat, then climbed in with her, setting the gas can on his lap. "You look nice," he said, giving her a quick once-over that made her toes tingle.

She hadn't paid much attention to what she'd put on this morning—a tank top and some jeans to be comfortable. "This is just what I grabbed."

"Maybe you should just grab every day."

"What? Wear jeans and a T-shirt to work?"

"No. Put on what feels right."

"Sure," she said, but it wasn't that simple. Nothing was as simple as Trip seemed to think it was.

They dropped the can off with the yard crew, filled the Volvo's tank at the nearest station and set off for the freeway.

"So, did you have fun the other night at that exercise class?" Trip asked. "What was it—Tae-Bo?"

"God, no. I basically got a leg cramp and spent the evening getting lectures about exercise and Orange Death."

"I beg your pardon?"

"Chee•tos. Known as Orange Death among health nuts."

Another chuckle. She loved making Trip laugh. She reached the freeway and sped up to merge with the traffic.

"So, was that Dave guy your date?" Aha. He was interested.

"I guess. Kitty thought he would help me get over Jared."

"And did he?"

"No. Actually, what helped me was you. And that talk we had on Valentine's Day." That talk and that kiss. "And maybe the ice cream." And that kiss.

"Really?"

"Yeah." Which made her wonder how in love she'd really been if one kiss had cured her hurt—even if it was the kiss to end all kisses. Which it wasn't, because she was quite sure Trip had more where that one came from. Maybe she was just in denial. Maybe she didn't have a clue.

Bingo.

"I'm glad I could help, then," Trip said.

"Me, too," she said, glancing at him, liking the feeling of having him in the car with her, close and companionable, his scent filling the space, his fingers on his knees, tapping time, looking like they wanted to move, maybe to touch her. Maybe she needed a refresher on that kiss... *Bad, bad Claire.* Maybe she needed a leash. More like a muzzle. No kissing, nipping or biting.

"It's nice that your friend Kitty looks out for you."

"Yeah. She means well, even when she's dragging me along against my will. Do you have good friends? With you moving around so much?"

"I keep in touch with people I care about. When I blow through town I stop in. And I make new friends all the time. Like you."

"We're friends, huh?"

"If you want."

"Sure," she said. "I'd like that." *Friends.* That was good. Really. Except being friends meant a big fat stop sign to anything else. Which was good. Ahem.

"Where are you from anyway? Originally? Where's your family?" If they were friends, she should know him better.

He chuckled. "I make you nervous, don't I?"

Absolutely. "Why would you say that?"

"Because you shoot questions at me like a detective. 'Mr. Osborn, can you account for your whereabouts on the night of fifteenth?'"

"Sorry." She grimaced. "You're just different from anyone I know, I guess." She glanced at him.

He was watching her with that wry expression, like he knew so much more than he would ever tell. "You, too, Claire," he said. "You're different from anyone I know, too."

"And that's a good thing?"

"Very good."

She let that hang in the air for as long as she could stand it, feeling heat rise up within her. "Except you know way more about me than I know about you. Hence the questions."

"True. Okay, you want my story. Let's see...." He leaned on the headrest. "I was born in Barstow and lived town-to-town in California with my mom when she had her act together. The rest of the time I stayed with other families."

"You mean as in foster homes?"

"My mom did her best, but let's just say she wasn't the most stable person on the planet."

"I'm sorry."

"Don't be. She's okay. I spend time with her in Colorado when I pass through." He leaned over to catch her gaze. "Don't paint any pictures of the poor foster kid with no one to love him. Really." He held her with his eyes, commanding her not to feel sorry for him, until she had to look back at where she was driving.

"The people I lived with were decent and kind. I got used to moving around. In fact, I like it now."

"That sounds pretty brave to me."

"In a way, I was lucky. I learned to sort out the things that matter from the fake stuff."

"The fake stuff? That a technical philosophy term?"

Trip chuckled, melodic and low, approving of her joke. "That's what I like about you. You're not just a pretty face—you're also a smart-ass."

She'd only made a joke to distract herself from what she was feeling for Trip. Attraction, sure. But also affection and admiration. He spoke so matter-of-factly about something that must have been traumatic to a kid, no matter how well-adjusted he'd turned out.

"And I like to travel. Next I head to New Mexico," he said, though she hadn't asked. "A novelist is offering a writing workshop I want to attend."

"That sounds fun."

"Yeah. And after that, I go to the Hopi reservation. I

met a guy whose grandfather is a shaman and he invited me to a festival."

"Sounds like a plan." Listening to him talk about moving on made her sad.

"Hey, don't worry," he said, patting her knee. "I'll be around long enough for you to get sick of me."

I doubt that. But she only nodded.

"So, is that enough about me?" he asked, giving her that sexy half smile. "You accept my alibi?"

"Not quite," she said, deciding to probe. "So, Mr. Osborn, is Trip your real name?"

"Oh, God," he said theatrically. "You won't be satisfied until you've pried every secret out of me."

"Don't make me get the bamboo for your fingernails."

"Trip is my real name," he said. "When my mom first saw me she was high on the pain meds they gave her for the birth, and she said, 'What a trip.' After that, it was a mystical thing—you know, the first words out of her mouth and all. And she thought having a kid was like a journey." He shrugged.

"That's kind of sweet."

"In a weird way. But I like the name. It suits me." For all his cheery talk, he seemed a little uncertain, a little sad.

"I don't mean to pry, Trip. I just like getting to know you better."

She felt him looking at her. She glanced over and saw his expression was intent and tender and thoughtful. "I usually listen more than I talk," he said. "But this has been okay. Nice, really."

"So, I can keep asking questions?"

"I don't know how I'd be able to stop you."

"So what about love?" she asked, ignoring his jab. "Have you been in love?"

"Maybe once." He sighed, sounding uncomfortable with the subject. "But that was a long time ago. And it didn't work out. I get too restless to settle anywhere with anyone, anyway."

"Sure. I see." But maybe with the right woman...

"How about you and love? Did you love the married guy?"

"I thought so, but now I'm not so sure. I kind of hope not because it turned out so...lame."

"You'll figure it out, Claire. I know it."

"How can you be so sure?"

"Because I know you," he said, his voice warm and intimate. "I'm your friend. And I just wish..."

She glanced at him. Their eyes met and held. Fire rose between them, hot and big. Trip wanted more than friendship, she saw, and he'd surely seen that in her face. They both jerked their gazes away, staring straight ahead. Claire squeezed the steering wheel with both hands. For a second, she could hardly see the road.

Neither of them spoke for the next few miles and they were soon exiting the freeway into Mesa. Claire broke the silence, pleased at how normal she managed to sound, by asking Trip to read the final directions to the halfway house. He sounded normal, too, as he navigated her to a brown-brick, Spanish-style house with a worn wooden sign saying New View House.

They climbed out of the car and walked up to two young men—ages nineteen or twenty—talking urgently over a battered road bike in the carport. Each held a handle.

"I gotta meet my probation officer in an hour," said

one, a white guy, overweight, with tattooed arms. "If I'm late, I'm jammed up."

The other man, a shorter, stocky Latino, shook his head, tugging the bike. "I signed up, Gordo. I need it for work."

"So take the bus."

"Too slow. I can't be late, man." The two men looked up at Claire and Trip. The white guy's expression said, *Yeah?*

"You two live here?" Claire asked.

The Latino nodded.

"I'm Claire Quinn with B&V Advertising, the company that's working on the ad campaign? Did Mickey tell you I was coming?"

"The Mick don't tell us shit we don't gotta know," the tattooed guy said.

"It's pretty new. I just arranged to come out a couple of days ago."

"You came to stare at the monkeys in the zoo?" the tattooed guy said.

Trip stepped forward slightly, as if to protect Claire.

But she didn't need protecting. "It's not like that," she said. "We want to encourage financial support for the house. I'm sure you can appreciate that."

"Yeah, Gordo," the Latino said. "The *chica's* tryin' to help us get enough bikes so I don't have to whip your punk ass just to get a ride across town."

The tattooed guy shrugged, seeming less irritated.

"So, can you tell me a little about what it's like here?" Claire asked the Latino.

Trip stepped back, confident she could handle things, she guessed. She liked that he didn't get macho and overprotective. He just supported her, silent and there.

"It's cool...except for the *pendejos* like Gordo here."

"Hey," Gordo said. "You're full of it, Julio." Claire could tell they were teasing each other. "My name's Ray, not Gordo," he said to Claire.

Julio snorted. "Yeah, you're not fat, you're big boned. Like Cartman on *South Park*."

Ray told Julio what he could do with himself in terms that made Claire blush, then continued, "We can stay as long as we hold down jobs and do shit—cooking, laundry, all that crap."

"And stay clean," Julio added. "No weapons and no fights."

"You mean, like over a bike," Claire said, lifting one brow in what she hoped they'd see as a teasing gesture.

"You got it, *chica*. See, hombre, she's telling us not to fight over this dog-doo set of wheels."

"So, what's good about this place?" she said, looking first at Julio, then at Ray. Mickey had told her the basics about the house—the residents were adult males and this was the last chance for most of them to straighten out their lives. "What would someone with cash need to hear to want to throw some your way?"

The two men considered her, then looked at each other. Their cockiness faded, their shoulders relaxed with thought. "It's kinda, like, open here," Julio said, glancing at Ray for his slight nod of agreement. "It's like they, like, trust you. Like they expect you to do good."

"The staff are a bunch of hard-asses," Ray said. "They watch you like guards."

"It's for your own good," Julio said. "You *need* a guard, man, to protect you from yourself."

"Eat me," Ray said cheerfully. "Gotta bug." He snatched the bike from Julio and rode off, moving with remarkable agility for someone so large. "Adios," he called to them.

"Hey, *pendejo!*" Julio yelled back. "Now I gotta get the stinkin' bus," he muttered to Claire and Trip, then started off at a strut, baggy pants low on his hips. A few steps away, he turned and called to them, "Go on in. The door's always open."

The words stuck with her.

Mickey, the house director, had a gray ponytail and sun-hardened wrinkles and he chain-smoked cigarettes as he explained how the counselors helped the men work through their bitterness, taught them to take responsibility for themselves, made sure they went to AA meetings and kept them talking things through.

There were setbacks and petty jealousies and honest heroics almost daily. Staff turnover was rapid, he told them, because the pay was low and the stress high. Some residents were powder kegs, but others only needed a listening ear and a boost to bloom.

He walked them through the house, showing them the wall-to-wall bunk beds in each room, the poster-covered walls, the human-heavy feeling of the place.

He introduced them to a few residents, who agreed to talk to Claire. The questions came easily, the answers more slowly, but as she talked, the men opened up bit by bit. She felt herself come alive. She felt purposeful, productive, part of the moment. The men picked up her enthusiasm and seemed to want her to understand.

She tried to memorize the phrases, the faces, the stories...

My big brother got me high the first time... I needed money... Had to have it or I hurt too bad... Robbed a liquor store... Spent time in juvie, then county... Broke my mom's

*heart... This place turned me around... A fresh start... I
turned my life over to a higher power... Don't give me that
twelve-step bullshit... It works, man. It's the only thing that
ever does.*

An exchange with one of the guys really stuck with
her: *It's like they know you can do it. Start over. Not get in
with the bad... Yeah, like the hand is out, and you just take it.*

When Claire climbed into the car after the four-hour
visit, she felt limp, but happy and more sure of herself
than she'd felt in a long time.

"You were amazing in there," Trip said, sitting beside her.

"Thanks." Her grin felt so wide she knew it must fill
her face. "I'm glad you were there, too."

"I didn't do anything except watch you be amazing."

Except it felt like more. It felt like she had a partner.

Claire's head was too full to drive home right away
so she pulled into a fast-food place and they bought
soft drinks and sat at an outside table. Trip fetched his
guitar from the back seat and tuned up, while Claire
took notes, filling four pages in a few moments. Trip
began playing a melody she'd never heard before. She
paused, midphrase. "That's pretty."

He nodded. "Something new."

"I didn't know you wrote music."

"When I'm in the mood," he said, still playing.

"I keep thinking about what that one guy said, 'Like
the hand is out and you just take it.'"

Trip strummed a few more chords, then sang,
"Someone held out, held out, a hand to me... Hand to
me..."

"Exactly," she said. "That's perfect!"

Trip smiled. "Let's see what else..." He played more,

then sang, "New view, fresh start, hands out…to have and hold…" He stopped. "No, that sounds like a wedding. Hmm…" He strummed more melody, humming and seemed to be considering more words. Abruptly, he played three quick chords with a flourish. "Done."

"Don't stop."

"That's what all the girls say." He waggled his brows.

She blushed. "I mean the song."

"That's it for now. I liked that place." He nodded in the direction of New View. "There are some brave guys living there."

"I know." She looked down the street, then back at Trip. Their eyes met and acknowledged their shared feelings about the halfway house…and maybe each other.

"I never got into drugs," he said.

"I didn't ask that."

"But I know you, Detective Quinn." They shared a smile over her grilling ways. "I knew kids who did. Some who didn't find a place in time. That's a great project, Claire. I'm glad you're doing it."

"See, working for an ad agency isn't completely corrupt and commercial."

"All jobs have their good points."

"But you don't approve?"

"It's your life. If you approve of it, who am I to judge?"

"Right." But did he approve of her work at B&V? "I don't know what I think sometimes. I have this picture of how I want things to be."

"Yeah? You mean the progress you were talking about?"

"Yeah. I sort of picture my perfect life." She laughed

at herself. "You know, the perfect career, the perfect relationship, the perfect me. You have to shoot high, right?"

"Unless that keeps you from enjoying now, this moment, which is all we really have." He tilted his head and leaned in, smiling a smile that she hoped he reserved for her.

"This moment seems pretty darn perfect to me," she said. She'd done good work and now the sun warmed the top of her head, a light breeze lifted her hair and Trip seemed to only have eyes for her. His sleeveless black tank displayed the swell of his muscles, the breadth of his shoulders. She liked the way the yin-yang tattoo emphasized his muscles. The sun glinted in his dark hair, which was thick and smooth and begging to be touched. And there was his mouth. Mmm. She'd tasted that mouth. Zing.

Whoops.

So much for the perfect moment. She couldn't let her attraction to Trip flare. They were friends. Just friends. If only she were as happy about it as Trip seemed to be. "We'd better get back," she said.

They got in the car and headed home. To keep her mind from straying into dangerous terrain, Claire talked through her thoughts about New View House, delighted by Trip's brainstorming skill and the easy way ideas ricocheted between them.

Every time their eyes met, though, Claire got another zing, which she tried to ignore. The effort wore her out, so that she was in knots by the time they finally pulled up to the guitar store where Trip wanted to be dropped off.

"Thanks for your help," she said, as he opened his door.

"All I did was watch you. And maybe keep the guys from hitting on you."

"Hitting on me? Hardly."

"You don't seem to realize how hot you are. Men watch you."

"I'm more of a background person."

"No way. You stand right out, bright and alive, like those brown-eyed Susans I gave you." His gaze followed her body up and down, intimate and affectionate.

A shiver traveled up her spine.

"Want to hang out a while?" he asked, sounding as reluctant to end the day as she felt.

She looked at her watch. Kyle would be at her place in an hour. "I'd love to, but I can't. I have—" *a date. Tell him you have a date* "—something."

"Of course. It's Saturday night." Was there a flicker of disappointment in his face? She sure as hell hoped so. "Dave?"

"God, no. Though he will be sending me a price list on his home gym, along with a free video and full-color brochure."

Trip smiled. "I'm so sorry."

"The date's with an accountant from our building. His name's Kyle."

"Kyle, huh?" He looked at her for a long moment. "He your perfect guy?"

"Too soon to tell."

"He better be great. To deserve you." He was out of the car in a flash. He leaned in the window, said, "See you," and was gone, leaving her with the usual questions: When and where?

"THE PLACE looks a little wild, I know," Claire said to Kyle, imagining the sight of her living room through his conservative eyes. Kitty's tiger sofa, leopard chaise and the nude drawings made the place look like a sex den.

"It's nice," Kyle said, his eyebrows lifted in an *ooh, la, la* motion. Before she could explain that the ambiance belonged to her roommate, the woman herself barreled across the living room wearing nothing but a camisole and matching bikini panties.

She saw Kyle and stopped short. "Oh, hi. Kyle, right?" she said, not even trying to cover herself. "I'm Kitty."

"Nice to meet you," Kyle said, shaking her hand, a little slack-jawed at the sight of her near nudity. "Kyle Carson."

"Kitty," Claire warned, giving herself an eyebrow cramp signaling for Kitty to scram.

"What?" Kitty said, reading her expression. "It's better than a muumuu, don't you think, Kyle?" she asked innocently.

"Oh, I would think so," Kyle said, sounding flustered as a freshman at his first strip club.

"Take good care of our Claire, will you? She's been in the dumps about her ex. So make sure she has fun— and I mean *fun*."

"You can't take Kitty seriously," Claire said, wishing she could get Kyle out of here before Kitty ruined her reputation altogether.

"Oh, I'm completely serious. All the time," Kitty said. "So you're an accountant?"

"That's what my W-2 says."

"That mean you always have lead in your pencil?"

"Twenty-four/seven," he said.

"Oooh," Kitty said, licking a finger and touching her

hip with a sizzling sound. "You did good, Claire. This one's hot."

"Thanks," Kyle said, rocking back and forth on his heels, pleased as a kid. Kitty brought out strange things in men.

"Don't let us keep you," Claire said to her.

"Oh, you're not," she said, prancing toward the kitchen.

"Wow," Kyle said, watching her go. "You two are great."

"Trust me, that's all Kitty. I'm not like that at all."

"Sure you're not," he said, his eyes twinkling.

Lord. He thought she was being modest. She grabbed her purse and dragged Kyle out of the apartment before Kitty could suggest a threesome.

6

THERE WERE PEOPLE in the elevator, so they rode to the lobby in silence. Claire was glad for the chance to secretly check out Kyle. He was tall and thin, but muscles swelled here and there, and he had a nice smile—maybe a little narrow, but spending all day adding up columns of numbers would thin anyone's lips.

She already liked him. After this evening, she expected to like him even more. No zing so far, but that was maybe because they already knew each other. Compatibility was way more important than chemistry in a relationship, according to Emily, anyway. Plus, the night was young. Plenty of time for pings and zings and fireworks to flare.

"That Kitty is something else," Kyle said as soon as they stepped out of the elevator. "I bet she's a handful as a roommate."

"Oh, yes. She keeps things lively."

"I'll bet." He seemed to ponder that thought for a second, then said, "So, enough about Kitty. How did you two meet?"

Lord. "We ended up in the same apartment in college. She kind of latched on to me and I thought she was fun."

"I bet you two had some wild times," Kyle said wistfully. "I was a bore in college. Always studying. Dullsville."

"That was a long time ago," she said. "And all your hard work paid off, right? You have a great job that you enjoy."

"I do love my work. True. I like making the numbers come out right for our clients. It's very satisfying."

"I know what you mean," she said. "When I get an idea the client goes for I feel like I'm on top of the world." This was good. They had something in common—a desire to please clients. And as they headed to a restaurant for dinner before the symphony in Kyle's squeaky clean Audi, she learned that he was as ambitious about his career as she was. They were very similar.

Claire's attention only faded for a second when they passed Ziggie's and she found herself looking for Trip's shape inside, her heart racing.

That was rude, so she tuned back in to Kyle, who was telling her an accountant joke. On top of all his other good qualities, he had a sense of humor. She felt even more hopeful.

Kyle guided her into the restaurant with a hand to her back. Still no zing, but his touch made her feel secure and appreciated. There was one awkward moment when he spent too much time calculating the relative dollar value of the wines on the wine list—okay, maybe he was a little tight with his money. But she could stand to be more frugal and he probably made wise investments with his savings—another good lesson.

The wine arrived and they raised their glasses. "To new adventures," Kyle said.

Adventures? That sounded a little overblown for a trip to the symphony, where it was doubtful they'd touch *Born to be Wild* with a ten-foot baton, but what the hell. Claire sipped her wine, then smiled. "Very nice."

"What's very nice is the chance to be alone with you for once," he said, then leaned forward. "Georgia and Mimi kind of take over at lunch."

"That's true. Now there are two wild women for you."

"No kidding."

They both laughed at that for so long that Claire had the panicked feeling they were running out of conversational topics. "That Georgia and Mimi," she said. They laughed a little more.

"They're a pair." More laughter, which trailed off.

"Anyway..." she said, scanning frantically for a subject. She was just about to bring up "those Phoenix Suns" or the weather, when Kyle said, "What I like about you, Claire, is that you know how to have fun." He looked at her like he expected her to do something outrageous—make the silverware dance or something.

"But I know how to be serious, too," she said. And it was high time she get that way.

"Why would you want to do that? Life's for living."

"But you can be serious and live life, too."

"I suppose so. Your work just sounds so fun and creative."

"It can be. Like, there's this project I'm working on..." She began telling him about New View House. He smiled in interest, and the conversational ball began flying easily back and forth.

Dinner over, they headed for Symphony Hall, where the concert audience was largely over the hill and the music subdued, but nice. The gentleman beside her dozed off twice—his wife thunking him each time he snored.

Claire's mind wandered to Trip playing his guitar at the fast-food place, then decided that was being disloyal to Kyle, who kept smiling at her, so she smiled back.

Such a sweet man. When she lost count of the movements and clapped before the end of the symphony—the sound ringing out, horribly wrong, heads turning to frown at her—he patted her hand kindly, not the least bit embarrassed by her faux pas.

Afterward, they drove home, laughing about the snoring man and talking easily. Except Claire couldn't help noticing there was no charge between them, even when they pulled into her apartment parking lot and the to-kiss-or-not-to-kiss moment was upon them.

Kyle put the car in park, then yawned.

"You're tired," she said. "I'll let you head home." She was out of the car before he'd even closed his mouth on the yawn.

"Wait, I'll walk you up." He *boop-booped* his alarm, and her heart sank. He expected a kiss.

Inside, Claire was saved from an awkward lip-lock by the sound of music blaring through her apartment door. Inside, she saw that Kitty was having a party. Claire recognized people from Kitty's real estate office, along with Rex and Dave, who was showing a video of his exercise equipment to a chesty blonde. Most of the dozen people were dancing.

"Spur of the moment," Kitty explained when Claire asked her about the gathering. Kitty teased Kyle into the middle of the room to dance and he launched into a weird thrasher step.

Claire smiled and nodded with the rhythm. When Kitty kept Kyle flailing through a second song, Claire tapped his shoulder, then rested her cheek on pressed-together palms to tell him she was going to bed.

He started for her.

"No, no. Keep dancing. Have fun. Stay as long as you want." She hoped he wouldn't throw out his back dancing that way. But at least Dave would be there to squeeze out any muscle cramps.

In her bedroom, Claire tried to read, but the party noise was too loud. Every now and then, Dave's voice rose above the din, talking about versatility, efficiency and payment plans.

She hoped Kitty wouldn't make a habit of late-night parties. On the other hand, at least Kyle was having fun. More fun, possibly, than he'd had with her. She'd enjoyed getting to know him better, but there'd been no spark. Meanwhile, the mere thought of Trip sent enough electricity racing through her to light a city.

Was it hopeless? Too soon to tell. She'd get the Chickateers' opinions before making any decisions.

"An excellent question, Kyle," Dave boomed from the other room. "Dollar for dollar, this is the best value on the market." On the other hand, now that Kyle had fallen into Dave's clutches, he might not want to have anything more to do with her.

CLAIRE USED ONE of the red Pick-Up Stix to flick off the green one, which flew across the table and into Kitty's lap. "Five points," Claire said.

It was Game Night, Claire's choice, the Wednesday after the symphony date with Kyle, and she'd chosen Pick-Up Stix as the perfect match for her life right now—a jumble of ideas, relationships and projects that overlapped and crisscrossed and needed to be delicately handled or they'd all fall apart.

"There was zero chemistry between you and Kyle," Kitty said to her, handing her the green stick. "Zip. Zero. Flat-line."

The truth of Kitty's words made Claire flub her next move.

"Meanwhile, you just blew Dave off," Kitty accused.

"He was not my type. There has to be a mental connection."

"At the very least, you could have gotten a free month of personal training. Not to mention a killer deal on a home gym."

"You can't date a man just to get exercise equipment," Zoe said, frowning at the mass of sticks. It was her turn. Her face was pale, Claire noticed, and she seemed preoccupied. Something was definitely bothering her. She'd ask about it soon.

"Chemistry is overrated," Emily said. "Mature relationships must be built. They don't just appear out of the mist of lust. You jiggled that yellow one, Zoe." Emily zeroed in on Zoe. "What's wrong? You're losing your touch."

"I guess I'm a little shaky tonight," Zoe said.

Satisfied, Emily looked over the tangled haystack of sticks, her plucking stick at the ready. "Marriage is a partnership. You have to be compatible." She tried for a stick too close to the prized fifty-point black stick and it jiggled. Emily tended to cut to the chase too soon.

Now it was Kitty's turn. "But chemistry is bedrock," she said. "If you're not hot for the guy, you might as well be sleeping with your brother." She slipped and moved two sticks.

"Ooh, ick," Claire said, going at the sticks again.

Abruptly, Kitty leaned close to her, over the mound

of sticks, and spoke low. "I know who you're hot for, Claire Quinn. Guitar Guy."

Claire jerked and a few sticks flicked into Kitty's face, while the rest rolled off the table into her own lap.

"Who's that?" Emily asked, while Claire collected the rolling sticks.

"He's a street musician who hangs near our apartment, playing for tips," Kitty said. "I had to drag her away from him for the date with Dave. Zoe, pay attention. You're up."

"Sorry," Zoe muttered with a wan smile.

"His name is Trip Osborn," Claire said, "and he's—"

Kitty interrupted. "Can you believe that's his name?"

"The name was his mother's idea. She had problems and—"

"He already told you about his mother?" Kitty said.

"A little. He and I talk when we run into each other. Actually, he, um, went with me to that rehab place Saturday."

"Ooooh. You didn't say word one to me about that. You are *so* hot for him."

"A married man isn't bad enough, now you're going for a street musician?" Emily said, so focused on Claire that she goofed her turn without even a curse word.

"He's a professional guitarist who's studying with a famous blues guy in town. He's also a graduate student." Sort of.

"In philosophy," Kitty added, taking her turn. "And Claire finds that *stimulating.*" She made finger quotes around the word. Then she goofed her move. "Damn. Your turn, Claire."

"But he makes a living playing music on corners?" Emily demanded again.

"He has other jobs," Claire said, deliberately missing so she could concentrate. She'd wanted to talk about Kyle, not her secret crush on Trip, so she was completely flustered. "He's kind of a student of life...."

"Oh, please," Emily said. "Zoe, your turn. Pay attention, hon."

"Maybe he'll teach you the guitar," Zoe said, removing an easy stick. She could have taken the black stick, which Claire had accidentally freed, and won the game, but she was settling for fringe sticks because she didn't care about winning as much as Emily and Kitty. Her usually steady hand trembled and the second easy stick quivered.

Kitty took over.

"If I asked him, I guess," Claire said. "We hit it off." *Do not mention the kiss. Do not mention the kiss.*

"Hit it off?" Kitty stopped hovering over the game and zeroed in on her. "Omigod! You slept with him!"

"Of course not! We just kissed." Damn. She'd mentioned the kiss. "Just once," she added quickly. "I went for ice cream on Valentine's Day after Jared didn't show and ran into him. He was so nice. I'd had too much champagne and it just happened."

"I knew it." With a flourish, Kitty flicked the black pick-up stick away from the pile. "Fifty points! I win! *And* I'm right about Claire. That should count double."

"Don't gloat," Emily said to Kitty, then turned to Claire. "This is not like you."

"Maybe it's exactly like me," she said, wondering if that might be true.

"You go, girl," Kitty said. "Musicians have great

hands. The calluses get rough, but if you use a good oily balm..."

"We're just friends, okay? Let it go."

"Kyle sounds like a good prospect," Emily said.

"He is sweet." Claire gathered the sticks and put them into their tube. "And thoughtful. And smart. And we have a lot in common and all. But I just don't get that feeling, you know?" She popped the lid onto the game and patted it.

"Feeling, schmeeling," Emily said. "You said you need a mental connection with a guy and you have that with Kyle. Question answered."

Kitty began refilling their wineglasses. Emily covered hers. "Watching carbs."

"Maybe you're not over Jared yet," Zoe said.

"Could be," Claire said. "So you think I should give Kyle more time?"

"Absolutely," Emily said. "You need at least four dates to test a relationship. Do different things—some fun, some serious. Don't you have the big B&V shindig coming up?"

"Yeah, I do. It sure would be nice to have a man with me. Kyle would fit in at B&V great. Everyone would love him and I would seem more...mature."

"You can't date a guy just to look good," Zoe said, chewing her lip in concern.

"Sure you can," Kitty said.

"Nobody's perfect, Claire," Emily said, frowning at Kitty. "Just get as close as you can. Trust me. I know this."

"I don't want to make a mistake is all."

"So stay clear of street musicians—stimulating or otherwise," Emily said firmly. "Kyle's a safe bet. Stick with him."

"Maybe you're right," Claire said.

"At least teach him to dance better," Kitty said. "Though he gets points for enthusiasm." She smiled an uncharacteristically tender smile, then poured more wine for everyone except Emily. "Here's to safe bets and stimulating guitarists," she said, lifting her glass.

They clinked goblets and followed with their "all-for-one, no sniveling" salute.

Claire noticed that Emily barely let the wine touch her lips. Diet or no, Emily never turned down her share of Game Night libations. A possibility dawned on Claire. "What's up with the not drinking, Em? Are you by any chance...pregnant?"

"God, no." Emily pinked. "But we're going to try soon, so I'm cutting out alcohol and taking more vitamins."

"Why would you do that now? Before?" Kitty said.

"To slough off anything that might harm the baby. The first three months are critical to overall health and development."

"Sheesh. You probably study for your eye exams," Kitty said. "Lord knows what you do for a urine test."

"Kitty!" Zoe said, slapping her gently. "Be nice. That's so exciting, Emily." She hugged her, though Emily stayed stiff.

"Barry and I have talked it over and the house is almost finished, so why not?" There was an extra brightness to her voice, a gleam of nervousness in her eye. Surely she wasn't getting pregnant just to keep busy? "Anyway, what's new with you, Zoe? Got any horoscope news to share?" Emily never asked about that stuff.

"Huh?" Zoe said, clearly lost in thought. "Oh, nothing new really."

Not true, Claire could see. "So how's rock climbing, Zoe?" she asked gently, guessing at the trouble.

"What?" She looked at Claire, then flopped against the banquette. "Awful."

"I thought after I went with you to that lesson you were okay with it," Kitty said.

"I took a little fall last weekend. I didn't get hurt, but it scared me and Brad had to help me down. He got bummed."

"*You* were scared, so *he* got bummed?" Kitty said.

"He was disappointed for me. And...well, things have been different ever since."

"He dumped you for being scared?" Kitty said.

"Take it easy." Claire shot Kitty a warning look.

"He hasn't dumped me. We've talked. A little. I know he's been busy at the bike shop. And there was a big ride to Tucson."

"That he didn't invite you on?" Kitty never let a thing rest until she'd ground the issue into the dust.

Zoe's features crumpled. "I just can't do it. I can't climb those rocks. Even for Brad."

"And you shouldn't have to," Claire said, hugging her friend. "No man is worth scaring yourself to death for."

"But we were getting so close. And I let him down."

"He let *you* down," Kitty said fiercely.

"You don't need that nonsense in your life," Emily added.

"But I love him," Zoe said.

"Say the word, and I'll sic Rex on his ass," Kitty said. "Wait, I know. You could date Dave. You like Tae-Bo, right?"

"Thanks anyway, Kitty," Zoe said, sitting up straighter. "Brad and I still have our bike trip to Mexico. And in the meantime, I signed up for a calligraphy class."

"That sounds good, Zoe," Claire said. "Take a class *you* like for a change."

"But I miss him," she sighed. "A lot."

"So call him up and give him hell," Kitty said.

"No. I'm going to stay centered and let what's going to happen happen."

"Again with the karma," Emily said. "I'm telling you, the Internet is the answer. There are tons of decent guys. And men for you, too, Kitty," she teased, "if you ever settle down."

Kitty gave a fake shudder.

Claire imagined herself doing things Emily's way. With pro/con lists and percentages. That was how Emily ended up with Barry. He was average everything. Not quite sexy or handsome or brilliant or ambitious. But Emily seemed happy, so maybe that was the way to go. What did Claire know? She'd gotten a crush on a passing musician and had to be convinced to date a sweet, sensible, compatible guy like Kyle.

She would give Kyle more time and try to stay clear of Trip. He just confused her—the last thing she needed with her emotions looking like the Pick-Up Stix game they'd just abandoned in favor of sniveling.

"BUT NEW VIEW HOUSE is such a visual story," Claire said to Ryan the next day. "The men are gruff, but profound, too. Real heartstrings stuff. A television ad is the perfect venue."

"No way will Biggs okay hitting up a videographer for the free work."

"But the print concept blends perfectly with the television one," she said, blocking her breasts with the print ad mockup she held on her lap to keep Ryan focused on the project, not her chest.

There's always a knee to the groin. Trip's suggestion popped into her head and made her smile. *Oh, I'm so sorry. I didn't realize your crotch was there.*

She should have asked a woman account exec to be her mentor—Anita, for example. But she always seemed harried and anxious to hurry home to her kids. Claire should have trusted her initial reaction to Ryan—that he had a thing for her. She always doubted herself.

"The ads are nice," Ryan said, reaching for them—so interested that he didn't even try an accidental breast brush. "You did a good job with the creative team. Sometimes they go for the easy idea."

"You should see the TV stuff we came up with—handheld cameras, close-ups of the men telling their stories, flashes of color. So striking." She needed Ryan's approval to bring them to life. "Can I at least mention the TV to Arthur?"

Ryan studied her, assessing her, but not in a sexual way. "You just don't quit, do you?" he said.

"How about if I get a detailed storyboard to you this afternoon?"

"Deal." He looked at her thoughtfully—not a speck of flirtation in his expression. "You're doing great, you know. You have good ideas and good follow-through. And you've taken the pressure off me."

"Thanks," she said, warmed by the praise. She'd earned Ryan's respect, at least, besides his lust.

Then he ruined it. "I'm looking forward to the party next week," he said in his honey voice. "You and I will be able to relax a little...not be so all work, no play."

Great. He'd probably sock back scotch and go for a

make-out session in the phone alcove. How to avoid that…? She had it.

"I can't wait to introduce you to my *boyfriend*," she said, pleased with her ploy. Okay, so she and Kyle had had only four dates and three strange kisses, but she needed *some* defense against Ryan's sappy looks and creepy hints.

"Oh," Ryan said, appropriately disappointed. "I didn't realize you had a boyfriend."

"Oh, yes. Yep. I do. Definitely. Indeedy."

Before he could ask for more details about her just-add-water boyfriend, Claire headed off to put the storyboard in play, a little queasy about dubbing Kyle her guy. Why? He almost *was*. And maybe should be. He'd probably like the idea.

So why didn't she?

"FROM HERE, you can improvise however you want," Trip said to the older of his landlord's sons. They were using a music computer program that included a keyboard and the kids were enthralled.

"I can just play whatever notes I feel like?" The kid's face lit up like a halogen lamp.

"If they're in the same key, yeah. Give it a try."

The kid dug in, his younger brother looking over his shoulder, dying for his turn. Trip would miss these guys when he moved out. Erik was right—there were some pleasures when you stayed around.

Maybe it was because they reminded him of the younger boys in his last foster home. The home that hurt too much to think about. But he'd been reliving snatches of the memories ever since that visit to the re-hab place with Claire. Maybe it was New View House.

Or maybe it was Claire. Something about her made him feel more. Notice more. Hell, want more.

He watched the boy plink away and let the memory play out. He'd been sixteen and they were living in Fresno when his mom lost her way again. He'd dreaded another foster home, but this one was special. The parents seemed to really care about him. And he loved their two young boys. The third son was almost his age and sullen, but he thought they got along okay. The parents encouraged Trip in school, bought him a new guitar, got him a job.

Without realizing how stupid it was, he'd relaxed, stopped feeling poised on the balls of his feet, ready to leave. He'd put his weight down, made plans, thought about what he'd do after graduation to make them proud. He'd hooked up with Nancy, too, and that made everything feel permanent and right.

He got so relaxed he didn't catch on to the oldest s's jealousy until it was too late and there was war. Tr handled the harassment when it was aimed at hi t when the kid started in on the younger boys bec hey liked Trip, that got to him. He wouldn't star tle kids getting picked on.

One hen the older boy forced one of his little brothers into a bike crash that banged him up pretty bad, Trip laid into the kid with both fists.

The family meeting afterward remained burned into his brain. He'd expected the parents to understand what had happened. When they said they'd asked social services to find him a new home, he felt punched in the gut. He could still taste the pain, like cold metal in his mouth, feel his insides crumple, his chest tighten so that he could barely draw breath, and the tears sting. He never cried.

They'd said the reason was that the foster mom's work was too demanding to give the family enough attention, but they couldn't meet his eyes, so he knew the truth. He'd made trouble, so he had to go. He'd been so shocked, so hurt, he'd actually begged for another chance. Even now he felt the humiliation of it. He'd known better than to fight. In foster homes, your job was to get along, to make things smooth, to make no trouble. He'd known that, but he'd thought the bond was there. He'd been stupid, ignored all the lessons he'd learned already.

He'd moved in with Nancy's family afterward—refusing another foster gig—hoping to hold on to something he loved, but he'd been too wounded and depressed, he guessed. When she accused him of being distant, he understood her to be right. He felt cut off from his mother, too—like a shadow, going through the motions, not ever really emotionally involved.

After that, he got back on his feet and moved on. Alone.

Oddly enough, to this day he still wondered about the foster family, still cared about them. Maybe he should look them up when he passed through Fresno again. He'd thought about California after New Mexico and the Hopi reservation. Summer was great in wine country.

Stick around and he'd end up feeling dead, he knew. He needed new horizons, new people and places to explore.

Except, whenever he thought about Claire, he had the urge to stay a while. Which was shortsighted of him, he knew. They were better off as friends.

Something about her made him want...more. Watching the way she reached out to the guys at the halfway

house, giving her heart to the moment, made him wish
he could do that. When he was with her he felt a connection he'd never felt before. An illusion, no doubt,
but a nice one.

"My turn!" the younger brother said now, shoving
his older brother so he almost fell off the computer
chair. Trip's attention returned to the computer music
program. His landlord shouted for the boys to get
ready, so they took off, after extracting Trip's promise
to return. He was happy to give it.

He headed out to the yard to practice a little before
he was due at Rosie's House for a lesson. Losing himself in music was always a pleasure.

Hummingbirds were going wild under the shade of
the desert willow, sucking at the orange trumpets of
honeysuckle. Bees buzzed, their movements as lazy
and sleepy as summer.

Trip began to strum the tune that had come to him
on Saturday with Claire. He liked how he felt when he
was around her—more aware, more alive—which surprised him because he prided himself on valuing each
moment. He loved talking to her, listening to her,
learning all about her. What a pleasure it was to see her
earnest eyes widen, her brows dip in concentration, to
hear her laughter or some smart remark or probing
question about his life. Maybe the questions had
sparked this memoryfest, this wondering about his ca-
pabilities. Interesting...

He sang the preliminary lyrics. "Hands...held out.
Hands out to me..." The words rolled out, the hummingbirds skittered and dashed around his head, reminding him of busy Claire. At the halfway house and
afterward, when they'd discussed the experience,
she'd been so *alive*. Sparking all over the place.

More lyrics came. He sang, smiling. Claire would like this. Maybe he'd play it for her. He could get there right about the time she came home from work. The thought of seeing her sent blood surging through his veins, reminding him that there was more to his feelings for her than friendship.

He remembered that look they'd exchanged in the car after they'd so sensibly agreed to be just friends. Pure heat had radiated between them, making him feel surprisingly out of control. Very new. And he'd kind of liked it.

What if they made love? Was there a way it could be okay? Maybe if they were clear about what it meant— momentary intimacy, a brief physical connection.

He shook his head at his stupidity. Claire was emotionally vulnerable and barely over her rat boyfriend. No matter what they agreed to, making love would open up possibilities Trip could never consider. And in the end, Claire would get hurt. And him? Uneasily, he pushed away the possibility that Claire might reach too deep, upset his basic understanding of himself, dig at feelings best left undisturbed.

"Hey, man."

He looked up to see Erik making his way across the yard. "You out here philosophizin'?"

"Just doing some thinking," Trip said.

"About that brown-eyed girl, I bet."

He chuckled. "You're downright psychic, my man. How come you haven't won the lottery yet?"

Erik joined him under the tree. "Let me see," he said, closing his eyes and pressing fingers to both temples, as if catching a vision. "You can't get her out of your head.... You think about her all day, dream about her all night...." He opened his eyes, grinning. "Better do something about it."

Trip shrugged.

"Jus' remember what I tol' you. Music ain't the only thing I know solid."

But Erik had it wrong this time. The best thing he could do about Claire—for both their sakes—was absolutely nothing.

7

"TRIP! HEY!"

Trip stilled, his hand on the glass door to Leonard's Market, and turned at the sound of the voice he'd been longing to hear for more than a week.

"Funny running into you here," Claire said, galloping toward him on the moonlit sidewalk, panting. More like running him down, but he didn't care. He was so glad to see her. His heart stirred, down deep.

"What a coincidence," she continued, gasping for breath. "I was just on my way for more ChocoCherry. Care to share?"

"Sounds great."

"We should go somewhere. My place maybe? We could get bowls this time and kick back and, um, talk?" She colored prettily.

Her place? Not a chance. There would be a bed there. Though the way he felt about her, he'd settle for the floor. "The citrus are in bloom over by the Heard Museum," he said. "We can sit in the moonlight and breathe in spring."

"Oh, yeah. Good idea," she said, disappointment flickering in her eyes. She covered it with a smile.

He held the door for her to enter.

"So, how have you been?" she said when she'd picked up the ice cream, letting the freezer door bang closed. He grabbed a couple of spoons and they headed for the cash register. "I haven't seen you for, gosh, almost two weeks."

Twelve days, to be exact. He had to laugh at himself. He could probably figure out the hours if he wanted to. "It's been a while," he said, pretending casualness.

"What have you been up to?" she asked as they headed for the cash register.

"This and that. Studying. Working on a paper. Teaching some music. I played at a folk festival at Encanto Park this weekend."

"I'd like to hear you perform," Claire said, her shoulder brushing him companionably as they headed out the door and started toward the museum.

God, he'd missed her. It was so familiar to walk with her beside him in the dark, her face lit by moonlight and the occasional streetlight. "There's a coffeehouse where I play a couple miles away, if you—"

"Name the date and time and I'll be there. Friends support each other."

"Yeah," he said. "They do." Except there was more than friendship at play between them, which was why he'd stayed clear of Claire's corner for the past twelve carefully counted days. Though he'd been haunting Leonard's like a lovesick ghost, hoping she'd return for this exact errand.

She studied him, wondering about his feelings, he could tell, which he did his best to hide. He was usually good at that. No attachments, no investment, no regrets. Only for some reason, on this beautiful spring night, he felt completely hooked. Tonight, Erik Terrifik's tips on finding a steady woman and learning her tricks hit home.

On the museum grounds, they found a spot on a stone bench under some trees. The moon was bright and inviting, the white blossoms so abundant they'd fallen and carpeted the grass at their feet.

Claire peeled the lid from the carton, and they dug in, their knuckles brushing, spoons colliding. They laughed and leaned over the carton. He loved it when her hair brushed his cheek, washing him with her perfume—something light and playful. He almost wished they weren't surrounded by the intense citrus smell so he could take it in and hang on to it, an olfactory treasure to savor later. What an idiot he was.

Claire was talking about ice cream and her three friends and how they played board games with themes and gave each other advice. He was only half listening because he was transfixed by her busy hands as they gestured and flew and waved and scooped. He wanted to grab them and pull them to his lips and kiss each finger and then her mouth, tasting ice cream and her own spicy taste.

She sat close enough that their legs touched. That and her open, eager expression weren't helping his composure one bit. His heart kicked into a faster rhythm. *You're losing it, pal.* But he was in no shape to care. He was busy figuring out an excuse to see her again. "I'll be at that coffeehouse Saturday night. Come hear me. We'll go for a drink afterward."

"Saturday? Oh." Claire's features sagged. "I have a thing...."

"A date, huh? Same guy?" Something stabbed his gut.

"Yeah. Kyle." Except she didn't seem very happy about it. And that made him unnaturally glad.

"Doesn't sound like you're looking forward to it."

"He's a good guy, and I like him, but when I'm with him my mind tends to wander."

"Not a good sign," he said too eagerly.

"We're just getting to know each other, so I figure I need to give it a little more time."

"You like him better than the bodybuilder, right?"

"Oh, yeah."

"He's not selling anything on the side?"

"God, no."

"But you're not quite sure he's right for you?" He tried not to sound hopeful. Hell, he wanted her to be happy, didn't he? Shouldn't he be rooting for this Kyle guy to work out?

"Yeah. He should be right for me. He's what I want...I think." She chewed her lip.

"Yeah? Tell me about your theoretically perfect man. What's he like?"

"You really want to know?" She looked at him, her brown eyes swirling with emotions—hope, confusion, pleasure at his interest and worry.

"Yes, I do." With everything in him, judging by the fact that he felt like a steel string about to snap.

She laughed, looked away. "Okay. My perfect man. Sheesh. That sounds so ridiculous. But you have to set your sights high, right?"

"Sure," he said with a sinking heart.

"Okay. I want someone who loves me, of course, and appreciates me for who I am. Someone mature, stable, financially okay and faithful, for God's sake..." She was referring to the married rat, he knew. Then she laughed, "You know, someone who likes sunset walks on the beach and mocha lattes over the Sunday *Times.*" She spoke in an airy voice, just playing now.

Trip smiled.

"That's it. My checklist. I know you can't fall in love according to a checklist or anything, but..."

"But that's what you want," he finished for her, catching her gaze with his. The familiar heat rose between them. The Stones song played in his head, about getting what you need instead of what you want. Maybe he was what she needed. For now.

"I guess," she said, but her lips parted and her eyes sparkled with desire.

He swallowed hard. "And this Kyle...he's all that? He's what you want?"

"Theoretically," she said, swallowing hard. "Except right now I want something different." Her voice shook and he saw a tremble wash through her body.

"You do?" he said hoarsely, aware of the pressure of her arm against his, the way her scent filled his head. God, how he wanted this woman. The feeling was raw and desperate and as deep and basic as his need for food or water or air in his lungs.

"Yes," she breathed, staring at him with those brown laser beams. "Right now, I want you." She put a hand on his shoulder and leaned in, tilting her head so their mouths would meet.

He whispered her name and got ready to capture those delicious lips, which would taste of chocolate and cherries this time, instead of mint and coffee. Below his belt, he was hard as stone, but inside he was liquid with wanting her. He was so close he could feel her breath against his face, sweet and warm and uncertain.

Why not kiss? Why not make love? Wasn't denying this power between them worse than having just a taste?

Because it was wrong, Trip knew immediately. Measured against Claire's checklist, he came up way short. She needed what she'd said she wanted—comfort, dependability, a long and steady love. All he had to offer were a few hot nights before he disappeared for good. And that wouldn't be even close to enough for Claire.

At the last second, he raised his aim and pressed a kiss to her forehead. "We can't," he said, fighting his body, which screamed that if they didn't, he'd explode.

Claire jerked away, her eyes wide with surprise and hurt. "Why not?"

"You should hold out for the man you want, Claire," he whispered, cupping her cheek. "And I'm not him."

"How do you know?" Her eyes searched his face.

"For one thing, I'll be gone in a month."

"So we have a month," she said, but he knew that was lust talking, not good sense.

"We're on different paths. We don't want the same things." He swallowed and delivered his closing argument. "You're giving Kyle a chance, remember?" The words caught in his throat.

He was painfully disappointed when she didn't argue with him. "You're right," she said, slumping, the light of desire fading from her eyes. "It's just that with you and me there's so much...so much..." She paused, looking for the word to describe what was between them.

He had a thesaurus's worth—energy, heat, hunger, craving, obsession. "Yeah," he finally said. "There's a lot between us. But it's not enough. Not for you. Not really. Didn't you tell me that you want progress? In your job and your life?"

"Why do you have to be such a good listener?"

"It's a flaw. What can I say?"

"You're right. I do want progress." She looked away.

His heart filled with a startling pain. He took a couple of steadying breaths. "Ice cream?" he asked softly, tilting the carton in her direction.

Mournfully, she scooped a spoonful.

He looked away to avoid seeing her tongue move on the cream in the way she had that made him want to throw her to the ground and make love to her on the spot. He had to clear his throat to speak. "So, how's the rehab project coming?"

"Fine," she said, giving a sad, shuddering sigh. "We came up with a terrific TV public service announcement." She kept talking about it. At first, her words were slow and heavy with sexual tension, but gradually she warmed to her subject and her pace quickened. Her eyes lit with the vision of it and her hands danced their ballet of enthusiasm.

Watching her, listening to her talk about the halfway house, Trip decided to finish the song he'd started for her. Just to make her happy. He loved making her happy.

And he would get the most out of what time they had together, too. He would enjoy her smile, her laugh, her energy and her ChocoCherry Rumba Swirl for as long as he could. That would have to be enough. Too bad he'd begun to want much more.

WHAT THE HELL was wrong with her? Claire asked herself, walking home wobbly as Jell-O, burning with frustration after sharing ice cream under the citrus trees with Trip. One minute she'd been talking rationally about how Kyle was the man she wanted and the next she'd practically thrown Trip to the blossom-covered grass and impaled herself on him.

It kind of irked her that he'd managed to be so sensible about it. He obviously wasn't as hot for her as she was for him. But where was all this heat coming from? Trip would be gone in a month and he wasn't the kind of man she wanted anyway. It had to be a symptom of something, but what?

As she walked, the answer dawned on her. Her insane hunger for Trip was due to her lack of desire for Kyle. Some kind of sublimation was going on. Her libido was rebelling against her determined efforts to hook up with Kyle.

The truth was that as much as Kyle fit her criteria for the perfect man, the chemistry was, as Kitty had said, zero, zip, flat-line. And chemistry counted for a lot, it turned out. Intellectual connection was vital, but so was chemistry. Or at least some sparks, for God's sake.

Now that she'd figured that out, she'd have to do something about it—stop seeing Kyle, first of all. To do otherwise would be leading him on. He was such a sweet guy and he'd been trying so hard. She hoped he wouldn't be too hurt. She'd call him tomorrow from work and tell him. Before the B&V party on Saturday...where he was supposed to be her boyfriend for Ryan Ames's benefit.

But that was less important than doing the right thing. She'd be as gentle as she could. He was such a sweet guy. He'd find the right person one day. It just wasn't Claire.

"I'M SURE you'll find the right person one day. It just isn't me."

"What are you saying?" Claire asked Kyle. The man was delivering *her* lines.

"I'm saying I think we should stop seeing each other."

"Okay...and tell me the reason again?"

"You have a great personality, Claire. You're funny and kind. But you're a little too serious, I guess. When we went to lunch with Mimi and Georgia, you seemed more, I don't know, spontaneous." A man who booked his vacations two years in advance was accusing her of not being spontaneous?

"I guess I thought you'd be more like your roommate Kitty. You know, more lively?"

"But I am lively. And spontaneous." She'd been toning herself down to be more mature—and for Kyle's sake, too. Meanwhile, the man probably wanted to make love in a glass elevator, run naked through the Civic Plaza fountain, drink milk out of the carton and see the dentist *ir*regularly.

"My counselor thought you would help me expand my emotional repertoire, but—"

"Hold it. Your psychiatrist told you to ask me out?"

"No, no. I couldn't afford a psychiatrist." He laughed in embarrassment. "My insurance covers six crisis intervention sessions and I was pretty flipped out when Leslie broke up with me, so I thought, why not use the insurance?"

"How sensible of you," she said on a sigh. So Kyle.

"I'm not what you want, either, though, right?" he said, anxiously. "I mean, there hasn't been much physical stuff."

"That's true." He was absolutely right. And she should be grateful that she wouldn't be hurting him, but it stung to see how fast and easy-breezily he was dumping her. She had her pride.

"I'm sorry to do this over the phone," Kyle said, "but I think sooner is better, don't you? Before we get in deeper and someone gets hurt."

Someone? He meant her. He was trying to let her down easy. Good lord.

"Will you be all right?" he asked gently.

Absolutely. The man kissed like a fish. "I'll be fine," she said. "Really."

"And I hope we can still be friends."

He was going for all the breakup clichés. Next it would be *It's not you, it's me.* But Kyle deserved some drama, especially since he'd been hurt by his last girlfriend, so she said, "I'm sure we can. It won't be easy, but I want that. And whenever I have trouble with math, I'll think of you."

"You're a wonderful person, Claire. Maybe if we'd met before I realized I needed to change, it would have been different. Just chalk it up to bad timing."

"Bad timing...right." More like *bad idea.* The truth was Kyle was the kind of guy she *should* want, not the kind she *did* want. Or need. She'd known it in her heart, she just hadn't trusted herself. She'd listened to Emily instead.

She got off the phone fast—before Kyle tried to line her up with some nice single guys in his office. Her only real regret was the loss of her instant boyfriend for the B&V party on Saturday. Today was Monday. Could she find a substitute in five days? Maybe she'd just tell Ryan her beau had been called away to perform emergency surgery. In Africa. If Ryan knew about her "breakup," he'd want to comfort her for sure. Double blech.

AT THE END of the day, Claire descended from the bus and headed home—hobbling because the defective heel of one of her new comfort pumps had finally snapped off while she was dashing for the bus. Just one more unfortunate episode in a day that had gone downhill after the Kyle breakup. Once she got safely home, she'd ponder it all and consider damage control.

"Hey, brown-eyed girl."

Trip's soothing voice washed over her like ice on a burn. Her whole body went soft with relief. She turned. "Am I glad to see you."

He glanced at his watch. "You're late—" then looked at her "—and you're limping."

"Yes, and that's the good news."

"Bad day at Black Rock?"

"The baddest."

"Tell me all about it." He put his arm around her shoulder and walked her to the broad stone banister where they always talked. She almost closed her eyes with the pleasure of it. They sat side by side and Trip scooted slightly so he could look into her face. "So, break it down for me. Start with your shoe. You use it to smack your mentor silly?"

"No. It snapped off when I was running for the bus, which I missed...which is why I'm late. Before that, I managed to blow my chance to impress Arthur Biggs with the TV idea."

"But you had that speech down cold."

"I know, but here's what happened. My stapler jammed and when I pried it apart, a staple flew down my blouse into my bra."

"Lucky staple."

"Quit it," she said, bumping him with her shoulder, liking that she felt safe to make contact with him. "It was poking me like mad, so I was fishing for it inside my bra. There I am, fondling my breasts, when in walks Arthur Biggs."

"Lucky man."

"This is serious."

"No kidding. Where's a videocam when you need one?"

"Trip!"

"Okay. What did he do?"

"He backed away mumbling that he'd get some coffee and come back."

"A true gentleman. So, did you get the staple out? And was it good for you?"

She gave him a fake glare. She loved how he was making her disaster seem comical. "So he comes back in with his coffee and sits down in my guest chair, and then Georgia yells to me through the phone intercom—'Lesbian lover on line three asking about the orgy on Saturday.'"

"Wow. A whole new side of you," Trip said.

"It was a joke, of course. And I say that to Biggs, but he looks embarrassed and says we can talk later."

"What did you do?"

"I ran after him."

"No. I mean about the threesome."

"Stop. I told Kitty I'd call her back."

"Let me know when you do."

"Do you want to hear this story or not?"

"Okay. I'll be good."

"An-n-nyway, I ran after Arthur, and when he turned around, my loose heel wobbled and I bumped him and coffee poured all over him."

"Ouch."

"Exactly. So, I tried to wipe it off with the hem of my blouse until I realized I was showing him my bra."

"Did he offer you beads?"

"So I steered him to the kitchen to clean him up," she said, ignoring his joke. "I apologized like mad, told him I don't usually take personal calls at work, and that I was glad he stopped by so I could explain an idea I had."

"Good recovery."

"Yeah, well, keep listening. I dampened a dish towel and started dabbing at his shirt and asked what he needed from me."

"After he'd gotten a shot of your breasts, what more could he want?"

"Trip." She slugged him. "An update on the New View project, he said, since the client would be at the B&V party on Saturday and he wanted to fill the guy in."

"A perfect lead-in."

"Exactly. So I started explaining, but the coffee wasn't rinsing off his shirt—he'd had cream in it—so I was thinking about dry-cleaning costs and losing my train of thought, and then I got down to his beltline and noticed there was a big wet spot around his zipper."

"Uh-oh."

"Yeah. Well, he must have thought I was going to start rubbing there because he grabbed the towel from me and said he'd take it from there. And he left."

"Was he angry?"

She shook her head. "More dazed, I think. I don't know if he even got what I meant about the TV PSA. I was just babbling."

"Then what did you do?"

"I wrote him an e-mail about the ad *and* offered to pay his laundry bill. But nothing. No answer. I don't know if he even likes the idea."

"Of course he liked it. It's great."

"I wish I were as confident as you," she said. "Now he thinks I'm a clumsy idiot."

"You can't help it that your shoe wobbled."

"Yeah, but that's the third thing I've spilled on the man. It's like I have some spillage karma or something."

"Maybe it's his karma."

"I did see him dribble a little at the water fountain."

"There you have it."

She smiled, feeling better. Just looking into Trip's smiling eyes lifted her spirits—and did things to her nerves. Here was all the fizz and sizzle she'd wanted with Kyle, but with an absolutely wrong man. And, she realized with dismay, the breakup with Kyle hadn't cooled the heat with Trip one degree.

"So, is that it for bad things?" Trip asked.

"Oh, no. Before that, Kyle broke up with me."

"He did?" Trip sounded almost relieved. "I'm sorry."

"It's okay. I was actually going to break up with him. He just beat me to the punch."

"That's good, then?"

"Except guess why he wanted to stop seeing me."

"He's an idiot?"

She smiled. "I'm not *lively* enough for him."

"He *is* an idiot." His words warmed her to her broken-heeled shoes.

"It's just weird. We should have been perfect together.... It doesn't matter. There was no chemistry."

"Ah, chemistry." Trip nodded, then looked at her. Their gazes caught and there was chemistry to spare— a big fat industrial laboratory with fizzing and hissing solutions, flaming Bunsen burners, shooting sparks and exploding experiments.

"Yeah, chemistry," she said, breaking the gaze. She took a shaky breath and tried to resume the joking tone they'd started with. "So, the breakup was a relief, except that Kyle was supposed to be my boyfriend for the B&V party on Saturday."

"Your boyfriend? You were that close?"

"No. One day I just blurted to Ryan that my boyfriend was coming to the party—just to fend him off, you know? Now, I'll have to try to fix my blunder with Arthur, while maneuvering around Ryan, who'll be dying to keep me company."

"That's a drag," Trip said, but he looked amused.

"It's not a big deal really." She sighed again. "The big deal is that I'm afraid I'll never get the love thing right."

"Sure you will, Claire. Once you stop looking so hard." His eyes met hers again and they were full of feeling. Which raised crazy hopes in her heart.

What if she'd already found it? What if true love just showed up on her corner playing guitar? She remembered the conversation under the citrus tree and how much she'd wanted him then. Only the idea of giving herself more time with Kyle had kept her from jumping him right there. They were on different paths, Trip had said. But Kyle was out of the picture now. What if their paths merged...and led to a bed?

"Too bad you have that party Saturday," Trip said. "I was going to ask you to come hear me play at a blues club."

"Damn," she said. "That's twice that's happened."

"There will be other times." He shrugged.

But how many before he left? "Don't give up on me, Trip."

"I never could," he said, his gaze deepening.

Heat rushed through her, making her want to squirm in her skirt. "So, that was my day," she said, trying to act normal while she sorted through these new thoughts. "Tell me about yours. You must have worked outside." He looked very tan.

"Yeah. In the morning, I trimmed palms with a crew, went for a swim, finished up a paper that's due, jammed with Erik, then headed over here to meet you."

"What if I'd worked late? I would have missed you. Give me a call next time, so I can plan on it."

Trip's expression closed down. "Let's just play it by ear."

Embarrassment heated her cheeks. He thought she was getting clingy, but she just wanted to be able to count on seeing him.

"Sure. That makes sense." She looked into his silver-gray eyes and decided she had to ditch this crush right now. Trip definitely didn't want her as much as she wanted him. And she was not about to throw herself at him. Not after Jared. Bigamy was humiliation enough for any woman.

If she ever wanted to get the love thing right, she'd better stop fantasizing about a guy whose very name sounded like a bad idea. After all, what came after a trip? A fall, of course.

8

"WHAT DO YOU THINK?" Claire asked Kitty Saturday evening, turning slowly in the elegant A-line dress with the velvet bolero jacket she'd borrowed from Emily for the party.

"Very sophisticated," Kitty said, applying her most intense fashionista scrutiny to Claire's look. "Especially the hair."

Kitty had done Claire's hair, pinning it up on her head—stabbing her in the scalp a few times in the process—and curling a few strands so they dripped down the sides of her face. Claire's cheek only stung a little where Kitty had accidentally dabbed the curling iron. She might be brusque, but she knew style.

"I do look perfect, huh?" Claire said, looking past Kitty to the mirror.

"Completely. Cool and classy." Kitty sounded as proud as if she'd chosen the dress herself. But Claire had picked it. And for once, she was confident she was dressed right. Come to think of it, ever since Trip had mentioned the idea of just grabbing whatever she felt like wearing, she'd stopped angsting over her wardrobe. A good sign.

"I agree," she said. "And I'll just glide over to Arthur Biggs, all cool and classy, and joke away that little staple-in-my-bra, coffee-on-his-crotch incident."

"Perfect," Kitty said, chuckling. She reached up to tug another strand of Claire's hair down.

"Ouch. Take it easy."

"Isn't this fun?" Kitty said. "We're finally doing our girl talk thing."

"Yeah, we are." And it was fun.

Kitty glanced at her watch. "I might have time enough to do your makeup."

"Oh, no. You've done enough already." So far her injuries had been slight. She didn't want to risk a mascara wand in the eye.

"You sure?" Kitty asked, clearly wanting the distraction.

Claire nodded.

"I should get going, I guess," Kitty said reluctantly.

"You going out with Rex?"

"Yeah. But only to break up with him."

"You're breaking up?"

"Yeah. We have to. We're getting bored with each other."

"We? Does Rex feel that way?"

"He's a guy. He doesn't talk about feelings. He just acts mopey and miserable. He'll be relieved, trust me."

"Maybe you could give it a little more time, see what happens. Maybe he wants more, not less."

"Please. Rex and I are about good times, not serious stuff."

"Okay." Claire did have a hard time envisioning the two of them sitting across the kitchen table from each other morning after morning with anything to say. "But you will get serious sometime, right?"

"Me? I don't know. Settling down is so...permanent."

"You sound like Trip. He claims nothing's permanent."

"He's probably right." Kitty glanced at her, then something on Claire's face made her do a double take. "You really like him, don't you? Look how red in the face you're getting."

"No. It's stupid." She gave an awkward laugh. "It's just a crush. Chemistry, like you said."

"I knew it! This is great. Let's eat something and dissect men for a few. Do this girl-talk thing right." Kitty tugged Claire to the kitchen. Claire sat at the table, while Kitty opened the freezer and removed the carton of ChocoCherry Claire had placed there after sharing some with Trip at the Heard.

Kitty peeled off the lid and looked inside. "All gone." She shrugged, untroubled, tossed the container in the trash, then began rummaging in the fridge.

The carton had been half-full when Claire had last seen it. Here was her chance to say something about Kitty leaving the empty containers in the freezer.

But before she could open her mouth, Kitty spoke, her head still in the fridge. "Looks like my liquid yogurts are all gone, too."

Ulp. Claire had drunk the last one and hadn't been to the store to replace them. "I think that's my fault. Sorry."

"Forget it. It's a roommate thing," she said, emerging with a pickle jar. She opened the jar and handed a garlicky pickle to Claire, then took one for herself.

Relieved at Kitty's easygoing response to her grocery crime—she might be better at this roommate thing than Claire—she joked, "Ice cream and pickles? You're not pregnant, are you?"

"God no. Knock wood." She slapped the penis-shaped vegetable on the table. "I just like the tang." She took a big bite. "In my men, too." She smiled. "So, you've got the hots for Guitar Guy... Tell Kitty all."

Claire bit the tip off her pickle. "There's not much to tell. He's not what I want."

"From the waist down or the waist up?"

"Stop it." She slapped Kitty's upper arm with her beheaded pickle. "I don't know what I want anymore. I'm taking a hiatus from men. Jared was a mistake and Thighmaster Dave a waste of time."

"No kidding. I just filled another trash bag with his exercise equipment promotional crap."

"I warned you."

"But if you'd slept with him, he'd probably have *given* us the equipment."

"Using a man to get equipment. Zoe would be scandalized."

"Good point. I'd rather use a man *and* his equipment." She waggled her brow.

"Anyway, back to me." She laughed. "Jared and Dave were wrong for me."

"And so was Kyle," Kitty said, crunching her pickle, then waving it at Claire. "That was so obvious. Now Trip...that's different."

"Not really. He's an escape valve, a distraction."

"Please," Kitty said. "Whenever you talk about him, your eyes go all sparkly, and you get twitchy and breathe funny."

"Really? Maybe I'm coming down with something." She widened her eyes in pretend alarm and checked her forehead for fever. "It's a crush, that's all."

"You are truly clueless, Claire."

"I'm taking Zoe's advice and letting whatever happens happen. A watched microwave never dings, right?"

"Go after Trip. See what happens. Where's the harm?"

"He's not the guy I want. It would be just sex."

"We've had this talk before. There's nothing wrong with just sex. Ten thousand nymphos can't be wrong."

"He's leaving in a month. And he doesn't want what I want." She paused, then confessed, "Besides, he's not as hot for me as I am for him."

"Is that it? He's just acting cool. You hit on him for real and he'll go for it. Believe me. I know these things."

"Maybe I'm just hot for him because he's elusive. He's probably right that it would be a bad idea."

"Don't give up so easy. You should trust yourself more, Claire. If you had, you'd never have gotten past the potato soup stage with Kyle. He is cute, though, I'll give him that." She paused, lost in thought—and her pickle—for a moment. "You need to stop listening to Emily."

"And start listening to you?" Claire teased. "Okay, maybe I will. But only if you listen to me. Give yourself a chance to get hooked on a guy."

"The guys I date? I don't think so."

"Exactly. Stop dating permanent bachelors. Expand your dating pool. Open your eyes to other guys."

"I don't know...."

"Trust yourself, like you're telling me to do. Who knows, you could meet Mr. Permanent at your next open house. Some single guy getting ready to settle down, buying a home, looking for Ms. Right..."

Kitty considered the idea, munching away. "I'll think about it." Then she smiled at Claire. "Isn't this fun? We're doing it all—fixing our hair, eating, dissing men."

"Yeah, it is." The curling iron burn only hurt when Claire smiled.

"I had my doubts for a while," Kitty said, "but you've turned out to be a decent roommate. Even when you use up too much hot water and bang around in the kitchen too early and make the coffee too weak."

"Oh, yeah?" She could mention the glass breakage, late-night parties and the jungle-sex noises in the middle of the night, but just then, Claire was pretty happy to have Kitty around. "You, too, Kitty," she said, tapping her last bite of pickle against Kitty's. "Here's to being roommates."

"Here's to you having sex with Trip," Kitty corrected.

"And to you meeting Mr. Right at an open house."

"Whatever." Neither of them, it was clear, planned to take the other's advice.

They finished up the pickles and Kitty took off to break up with Rex. Claire returned to the bathroom to do her makeup. She was penciling in her lip liner when her apartment buzzer sounded.

She hurried to the intercom, holding her pencil aloft. "Yes?" she said into the box.

"It's Trip."

"Trip? What are you doing here?" It was as if she and Kitty had conjured him up.

"Can I come up?

"Up here? To, um, my apartment?"

"That's the general idea." There was laughter in his voice.

"Oh, sure. Of course," she said, gathering her wits.

He'd never been inside her place. She felt suddenly exposed. And very happy.

When she opened the door, the way Trip looked made her knees go weak. He wore a gray tweed jacket over a black silk, scoop-necked T-shirt and black slacks. He looked very hip and devastatingly handsome. His guitar rested on the floor at his feet. He held its strap in fingers that seemed...nervous. Unusual for a guy who always seemed cool and calm.

She stepped back, inviting him to enter.

"Rent-a-boyfriend at your service," he said with a salute.

"Rent a what?"

"I'm going with you to your party."

"You're kidding."

"You need a boyfriend to help you fend off your mentor, right? Plus I can keep you from pouring wine on Biggs. Or at least make sure it's white wine—no stains." His apparent embarrassment touched her.

"But don't you have a gig?"

"I got someone to sit in for me. Money's money, but a friend in need...that's big." He held her gaze, not even looking around at her apartment, which he'd never before seen. She couldn't take her eyes off him, either.

The time stretched. Heat rose like a tide up from Claire's feet and out through her fingertips. "You look great," she said. "Or should I say, 'Nice getup'?" The joke—referring to their first meeting when he'd criticized her suit—felt safer than what she felt like saying, which was, *Kiss me, take me, make me forget my name.*

"You look gorgeous," he said. "Your dress...your hair..." He assessed her in a way that sent a tremor through her. Then his brow dipped in curiosity. "Except something's wrong with your mouth there." He moved forward as if to touch her lips.

She realized she'd only done one lip and her liner stick was upthrust in one hand. Just like with the one-eyed mascara smear the night of the ice cream run, she looked lopsided and goofy to him. "I'm not quite ready. I'll, um, be right back." She stood frozen in place.

"You do that," he said. "I'll be right here."

"Sure, sure," she said, not moving. Trip was coming with her to the party? As her boyfriend? That was so helpful and thoughtful. So why was her stomach in a knot?

Because this would be weird. Trip had nothing in common with the B&V crew and clients. "I should warn you it'll be a bunch of advertising people. The partners can be pretentious and the account execs are materialistic and shallow. The clients are a mixed bunch. Not to mention the designers. You'll be bored stiff."

"I'll be with you. How can I be bored?"

"That's sweet, but..."

"Go get ready," he said, shooing her away.

She turned and headed for the bathroom, realizing that what Trip thought about B&V wasn't her only worry. What would B&V think of Trip? A student-street musician wouldn't exactly make her seem mature and upwardly mobile. But that was being as superficial as she'd just declared the B&V crowd to be.

Was she a superficial person? Being in advertising trained you to attend to appearances, all right. But she had more depth than that, didn't she? She'd think about that later. She had enough to handle with a handsome musician waiting in her living room.

She penciled in the rest of her mouth and returned. Trip was still there—he hadn't disappeared in a puff of smoke—looking smooth and cool and comfortable in his clothes. He threw his guitar over his shoulder and headed for the door.

"You're bringing your guitar?"

"I might feel like playing," he said, smiling mysteriously, holding the door for her.

Not on any corners, she fervently hoped, then chided herself for being a snob.

They caught the downtown bus, which was nearly empty at this time of night, and got off a block from the Hyatt, where the party was being held.

The B&V reception filled the smallish room, which buzzed with conversation. Claire surveyed the crowd of account execs, clients and their spouses, secretaries and clusters of creative teams.

Georgia's smoky honk burst out—Mimi must have told a dirty joke. Claire would love to join that group, but she had bigger fish to fry. She spotted Arthur Biggs and Carlos Vega holding forth in the middle of the room, surrounded by the top AEs and big clients. How would she slip into that tight knot of power with her joky speech?

Just wanted to touch base about the New View project. I don't think you caught the flavor of the campaign, what with all the coffee dabbing and brassiere-flashing.... She couldn't be flip with important people listening in. She had to get him alone or something.

"So, let's start with the food, huh?" Trip said, indicating the two sweeps of skirted tables overflowing with shrimp, veggies, rumaki, tiny tamales, stuffed grape leaves, spanakopita and more. He leaned his guitar against the end of a table and began loading a glass plate with food. Lots of food.

She joined him, choosing a few items. She noticed that most people had little dabs of food on their plates, while Trip's groaned with stuff. "You must be hungry," she said, a little embarrassed for him.

"Hey, free eats," he said. "Gather ye calamari while ye may." He put an entire puff pastry into his mouth. He wasn't being a slob. Just eating with gusto. Eating a lot. And with lots of gusto. "If only I'd brought baggies for the leftovers."

"Trip!"

"Just kidding. Relax. Eat something. You're a stick."

But Claire's stomach was too jumpy for food. Maybe a glass of wine. "Shall we get something to drink?" she said, putting her untouched plate on the wait tray.

Trip nodded, still chewing.

As they approached the bar, Claire spotted Ryan. "Ryan!" she called to him, elbowing Trip to get his attention. "Nice to see you."

Trip took in a dolma in a single bite, swiped his fingers on the napkin Claire extended, then shook Ryan's hand.

"Ryan, this is..." She hesitated. If only his name were more dignified than *Trip*.

"Trip Osborn, Claire's boyfriend," Trip said firmly, making both his name and their relationship sound solid and certain. Relief and pleasure washed over her.

"Ryan Ames," Ryan said, taking Trip's measure along with his hand.

"Oh, yes. Claire's mentor," he said, putting his arm snugly around her. "I've heard so much about you."

"All good, I hope," Ryan said...sounding nervous.

"What else could it be?"

A perfect touché. Pink slid up from under Ryan's collar.

Trip tugged her even tighter against him. "I know she appreciates all that you're teaching her."

"Actually, Claire's taken the lead on the project," Ryan said, surprisingly gracious and sincere sounding. He smiled.

"That doesn't surprise me," Trip said. "Claire has a lot to offer. She's smart and creative and energetic. She'd be an asset to any place she chose to work."

"Trip, please," she said, blushing to her roots, but loving it anyway. "You sound like my agent."

"It's all true," he said, leveling his gray eyes at her. Then he looked back at Ryan. "Anyway, I'm glad to finally meet you. And your wife?" He pretended to look beyond Ryan for the missus, his eyes twinkling with mischief. "I want to personally thank her for letting us borrow you all those extra hours."

"My wife? Oh, no, she's not here." Ryan went bright red and shifted his weight in discomfort. "These events bore her."

"That's a shame," Trip said. "It's nice when you can share things with your spouse. And you have children, right?"

"Yes. A boy and a girl." Ryan brightened, looking like the man Claire had liked before she asked him to be her mentor and he started slobbering at her.

"That must be an amazing thing," Trip said. "Having kids makes everything so much more important."

"That's true," he said thoughtfully. "You want the best for your kids."

"Do you have pictures?" Trip asked.

"Absolutely." He whipped out his wallet and

flipped open an accordion fold of shots faster than he pitched ideas. And that was fast.

Trip admired photo after photo and asked questions while Ryan told them about his son's skill in soccer, his daughter's talent with piano. "You're a lucky man," Trip said, as Ryan put his photos away. "Don't ever take your family for granted." There was a ferocity in his voice that told Claire he was speaking from his experiences as a foster kid with a flaky mother. That made her heart ache for him.

"You're right," Ryan said. He seemed to sense how strongly Trip meant the words. "Completely right. And sometimes I guess I do take them for granted."

Claire couldn't believe how masterfully Trip had put Ryan on the spot and reminded him what counted in one easy chat. She should never have doubted him. So what if he chowed down on hors d'ouervres? He knew how to handle himself with people.

"I don't think Claire mentioned what you do?" Ryan said.

"He's a musician," Claire said quickly, before Trip was tempted to say, *I trim palm trees* or *I'm a student of life.*

Trip flashed her a look of surprise. She hoped she hadn't hurt his feelings.

"He's very good," she continued. "He plays around town. In fact, he had a gig tonight, but he gave it up to come with me."

"So, that guitar is yours?" Ryan tilted his head at where Trip had left his case. When Trip nodded, he said, "Maybe we could give you a chance to play for us," as if he were offering Trip a shot at stardom.

"Trip's not working tonight," she said, squeezing him around the waist, loving the sensation, even as she ached with embarrassment. "He's here to support me."

"Sure, of course," Ryan said, his eyes roving the room. He was ready to do more schmoozing, she figured, now that his flirtation plans had crashed. Ryan was a climber, always working the angles, seizing every opportunity to move ahead. He'd given her tips along those lines, but she didn't really want to be like him in that way, she realized. She wanted her work to speak for her, not her skill at manipulating people.

"Here come the partners," Ryan said, his voice low and urgent. Sure enough, Arthur, Carlos and their entourage were headed toward the bar. "Go ahead and talk to Arthur about New View. He's feeling generous, since I got Sedona Sunset to double its budget. We may be able to pitch the television ad."

She hadn't told Ryan about the coffee spill of two days ago when she'd flubbed her first attempt to do that.

"Arthur!" Ryan called as he passed.

Arthur stopped, spun their way with a smile, then signaled the bartender for a refill with a lift of his empty highball glass, which he set on a table. The high-powered group swirled around Ryan, Claire and Trip, bringing the sweet smell of cigar smoke and the woody aroma of dark liquor. Claire's stomach jumped with anxiety.

Arthur put his half-gone cigar between his teeth and shook Ryan's hand, closing one eye against the smoke. "Ames," he said. "Good to see you... And our Claire," he added. He grinned and took a giant step backward. "Just staying out of range."

"I'm so sorry," she said. "Did you get my e-mail?"

"Just a little joke," Arthur explained to the gathered

crowd. "Claire considers unspilled liquid to be a personal challenge."

The group chuckled. Claire decided to seize the moment. "Put down your drinks and no one will get hurt," she said, pretending to hold a gun on the group.

Everyone laughed. Score one for cool, classy, upward-climbing Claire, mistress of cocktail repartée.

"I'm glad I've got you two together," Arthur said. "I want you to meet Winston Greystone and his wife Loralee." He indicated a portly, sixtyish man and a tall, chesty blonde half his age.

"Winston, this is the team I've got working on the New View project. In fact, Claire, why don't you lay out the concept for Winston? I was a little distracted when you explained it to me the other day."

Distracted? He'd been sopping wet. "Certainly." Here was her chance. For a second, Claire's throat locked up. She was going to have to describe her idea in front of all the B&V heavyweights, plus the Greystones. She'd rather do it while wiping coffee from Arthur's monogrammed shirt...or even his groin.

Trip must have sensed her tension because he placed his hand in the middle of her back. *You can do it*, he seemed to be saying. Warmth rushed through her from where he touched her. She took a deep breath and began to describe the print ads, with their theme of hands reaching out. She didn't dare mention the TV spot in front of the Greystones without Arthur's up-front okay.

Trip's hand dropped from her back, and she was aware that he'd moved away from her, but the feeling of warm support stayed with her.

When she finished, Winston Greystone spoke first. "Intriguing," he said. "You've correctly surmised that the story is in the people. I had hoped you'd consider a television component. I think TV is where we want to be."

"TV is an option," Arthur said, "but we believe the target audience will be effectively reached through print and radio. Billboards are also an option."

Winston frowned. "That's not what I was hoping for."

Claire looked at Ryan, who gave her a slight nod before he said, "We have sketched out a video concept we might consider...."

"Yes, we have," Claire added. "And it's quite good."

"Why don't you tell us about it?" Arthur said with a resigned sigh.

"Here's how it would open..." Claire began, wishing like anything she'd brought the actual storyboards. She pictured the PSA in her mind and tried to describe it. Except the crowd intimidated her and she left out a part and had to backtrack. She'd just stopped for a breath, her heart pounding, fearing she was blowing it, when a guitar began to play.

She turned, along with everyone else, and saw Trip tuning up a few feet away, his fingers quick and strong on the instrument. He looked up and smiled. "I think this might help you get a feel for what Claire is talking about," he said to the gathered crowd.

His silver eyes, like liquid metal, zeroed in on her, then he walked forward until they stood side-by-side, facing the crowd. He began to play the melody she recognized as the one he'd written the day they'd visited New View House.

After a few bars, he sang the lyrics she remembered, except they were better, more touching, more evocative. His golden voice filled the room, washing over them. *No one ever...no one ever there for me...there for me...before... Hand out to me. Hands free...for me... A place, a space, growing up...growing out.* He paused, hummed a little, then sang a chorus and finished with, *I'll get there, thanks to hands. Hands out...hand to me...for me... Hands.* The words were perfect.

There was a moment of awed silence and then everyone clapped, loud and long.

Trip tilted his head forward in thanks. "Why don't you go through it again, Claire?" he said, still playing, but more softly. So Claire described the ad again—better this time with Trip's music a soft soundtrack to her words, supporting her like Trip's hand on her back. When she finished, the applause was even louder than for Trip alone.

"Remarkable," Winston Greystone said. "Captures the place exactly. Very emotive. Powerful."

"I love it," Loralee said, her eyes on Trip.

"Nice work," Ryan muttered in Claire's ear. She didn't have a chance to explain that Trip's playing had surprised her, too.

"You're the composer?" Arthur asked Trip, shaking his hand.

"This is Trip Osborn," Ryan said, rushing forward. *Be at the center of things. Facilitate important contacts.* Ryan practiced what he preached, all right.

"I just love guitar," Loralee Greystone gushed to Trip. "Will you play more for us?"

"I don't know..." Trip said, his eyes asking Claire.

Pleasing the agency's top client's wife would garner points in the partners' eyes. "Would you mind?" Claire asked.

"No problem." Trip smiled, but the tension on his face said he didn't really want to play.

"Can we get something set up?" Carlos Vega said to a waitress standing nearby. "A stool, whatever?" He zeroed in on Trip. "What do you need?"

"A stool's good," Trip said. "Maybe a mic."

While this got arranged, Winston Greystone turned to Arthur. "I'd like to see this young lady's idea come to life, Art. Using that song. Like that recycling ad with that country star...I forget his name...."

"This is a local project, Winston. I can't imagine a celebrity being interested in—"

"Use the songwriter," he said, nodding to where Trip was getting situated on a bar stool on a small parquet area, almost a dance floor. "Live, of course. To get that energy. Down-to-earth, but arty. Funding New View House will seem like a bandwagon a corporate giving committee will want to be on." Obviously, Winston Greystone had picked up some Madison Avenue lingo.

"It's a great idea," Arthur said, "but to be perfectly honest, Winston, we don't have the budget."

"Dig down a little, Art. It's a good cause," Winston said. "How much business do we give you these days?"

"We'll work it out," Arthur said, clearing his throat.

"Very good. Let us know when the shoot will be," Winston said to Claire. "Loralee will want to be there. She does love guitar players." He smiled indulgently in the direction of his wife, who was motioning him over to where she stood with Trip.

Winston left and Arthur sighed.

"I didn't mean to put you on the spot," Claire said to him. "I hope I didn't do the wrong thing."

"No, no. It's good to have a rabbit in the hat. He would have pushed for more anyway. That's just Winston."

"I think it went well," Ryan said.

"Talk to Video Voice about donating one day's shoot," Arthur said to him. "On site. They owe us for the referrals to L.A." He turned to Claire. "Get your boyfriend out there. Loralee loves him." He rolled his eyes, then looked at Ryan. "What we do to keep Greystone Properties happy, eh?"

"Nature of the biz," Ryan said.

The reality of what had happened sank into Claire's awareness. "You mean we're doing my ad?"

Arthur smiled at her. "Yes. We're doing it. Have you ever produced a spot before?"

"Um, I was on site a couple times," she said. She'd been a gofer when she first started at B&V.

"I'll keep her on track," Ryan said. "Don't worry."

Arthur looked at Claire dead on. "I don't like to be muscled, Claire. No matter how charming the muscler. Don't make me regret this."

"You won't, sir. Absolutely not. It'll be perfect."

It had to be.

9

CLAIRE WATCHED Trip position himself to play, one heel hooked on the bottom rung of the stool, the other extended to the floor. Light from above spilled directly down on him, as if he were on a real stage under a spotlight. He looked like a star, too—sexy and confident, his hair gleaming in the light, with that celebrity aura that made an audience melt.

She was melting, all right. And tingling with pride...and a desire she'd rather not think about.

"Attention, everyone," Carlos Vega said. "Can the Muzak, would you?" he called into the air, as if to God. Obediently, God—or rather a harried waitress—cut the piped-in sound. "So," Vega continued, "we're about to be entertained by...Trent, is it?"

"Trip," he said. "Trip Osborn."

"Oh, right. Okay, then. Ladies and gentlemen, Biggs and Vega are proud to present, for your listening pleasure, Mr. Trip...um..."

"Osborn," Trip said again, not seeming the least bit annoyed by Vega flubbing his name—twice. He swung into a breathtakingly complicated jazz piece that had people murmuring in delight and awe. When he finished, the applause was sharp and loud. He nodded his thanks.

"I'm glad to be here tonight to help Claire." He smiled at her, his eyes holding her, offering her this gift of his time and talent, and she smiled back her thanks, feeling everyone's eyes on her.

"I understand you're all in advertising, so here's a little medley you'll enjoy. See if you recognize this." He started with the song from the current Mitsubishi car commercial. The audience clapped in recognition. Then he moved into the song for a major insurance company, a floor cleanser and an antacid. When he started on a series of McDonald's theme songs, he urged everyone to sing along.

So people sang through several more famous commercials. When he finished, the room rang with applause. Claire was sure he meant the montage as a jab, but no one seemed offended.

"He's good," Ryan said to her. "Very good."

"He is, isn't he?" she said. Strange that she was finally hearing Trip play for an audience and it was for her work. For free.

"Now, for something completely different," Trip said and began an instrumental blues song. Light glinted off the metal and polished honey wood of his guitar, and he played with his head tilted forward, leaning into the guitar as if to catch secret notes no one else could hear.

He gave off an energy that was very sexual. His fingers were graceful and loving and seemed to coax out the notes, as if he were making love to the instrument and the audience at the same time.

He raised his gaze and made eye contact with each person in turn, inviting each to indulge him, enjoy his music, his gift.

And they loved him, she could see. Everyone was engaged. People she knew to be jaded, neurotic, stoned or silly were rapt and smiling, caught in the moment, absorbed in Trip's music, his flying fingers.

This was the real Trip. He'd arrived at her place in a costume to play a role for her, but at this moment, playing the music he loved, he was deeply real. Solidly himself. It didn't matter how he was dressed, either. If he'd been standing there in a ragged T-shirt and paint-smeared cutoffs he'd still be weaving his magic. She wished she had his self-assurance.

Tonight she'd been acting the part of mature ad executive in her formal dress, upswept hair, with her serious boyfriend. She still was. When did *she* feel real...true to herself? When she'd explained the ad. She'd felt solid then. And when she'd visited New View House. And whenever she was with Trip. With Trip she felt very real.

He moved into some jazz standards—Ellington, Porter, others. Someone called out "My Funny Valentine," which he played looking directly at Claire. His voice was smooth as silk, as liquid as his gray eyes. She felt everyone's gaze on her and went warm all over. They all thought Trip was her boyfriend, that he'd chosen her.

And just then, that's exactly what she wanted. She wanted him to be her boyfriend. If Kitty was correct, if she made a move, Trip might join her in the moment. Tonight, she was willing to risk it. He kept saying he wouldn't be here long. But maybe it would be long enough. And maybe he would decide to stay.

Warmed by the thought, she grinned as Trip motioned Mimi and Georgia up to join him in singing "Sentimental Journey" as his finale. Georgia's hoarse rasp was a decent harmony and the trio sounded almost professional.

When the song was over, people laughed and clapped and whistled, while Trip pushed off from the stool. "Thanks, folks. That's it for me. Unless..." He lifted up his empty wineglass and wiggled it as if it were a tip jar. Everyone laughed. Only Claire knew how close that was to the truth.

He walked toward her. With everyone watching, Claire had no choice but to throw her arms around him for a hug. Trip seemed pleased and prolonged the embrace with one arm—his guitar hung from his other hand. She buried her face in his neck, damp with sweat and smelling wonderfully of him.

"How did I do?" he asked, his eyes telling her he already knew, but he wanted to hear it from her.

"You were amazing," she said. "Absolutely amazing."

"That was my plan."

"And thanks to you, they're going to do my television spot." She looked into his face.

"That's good, then."

"Your song sold the idea. Without you, it wouldn't have happened."

"I just gave you a boost, Claire. You don't realize how good you are."

His praise pleased her, but she had to tell him about his critical role in the project. "The thing is that they want you in the commercial. Playing. Isn't that great?"

"They want me?" His eyes flickered away. "I don't know. That's not really my thing."

"But it's crucial, Trip. The Greystones want you, so Arthur wants you. You'll do it, won't you? Please?"

His gaze returned to her face, reading her urgency. "If it means that much to you."

"It means a lot," she said, sensing his reluctance.

"Okay, then," he said.

"And you mean a lot, too." The heat between them intensified—but too quickly and publicly. "Let's get a beer."

All the way to the bar, people stopped them to congratulate Trip on his skill and Claire on her taste in boyfriends. She basked in the glory of it. She'd definitely made a good impression on the powers that be.

They'd made their way to a table, tapped their beer glasses and looked at each other, their eyes filled with emotion. Emotion Claire wasn't ready to share. "You were making fun of us with the commercial jingles, weren't you?" she asked, then sipped her beer.

"In a way." Trip took a drink, too.

"But everyone loved it."

"Why wouldn't they? Commercials are their bread-and-butter."

"Mine, too, but it bothered me some."

"That's because you have doubts. They don't."

"Everyone questions themselves. Don't you?"

"Not about the basics. I'm pretty sure about me and what I want."

"Maybe you're too sure. Maybe you could learn from someone else." She paused, watching him, cheered by the flicker of hesitation in his eyes. "I learn from people all the time. My friends...and you."

"But you have to trust your inner compass." He tapped her high on her chest. "You can't turn over the wheel to someone else and let them drive."

"And you," she tapped him in the same place, "can't shove every new idea into the back seat and ignore it."

"Good point," he said, his gaze heating. "Maybe I should consider other...options." His eyes roved her face, focusing on her lips.

"Yeah...options."

"You make me want to," he breathed, leaning in, his words low, intense, his breath warm. "Do you know how tough it is for me to sit here pretending to be your boyfriend, knowing that when we walk out of here it will be all over?"

"I know exactly how you feel," she said, holding his gaze, praying the spirit of Kitty would stick with her. "But what if it wasn't over? What if you were my boyfriend? For real?"

He opened his mouth—probably to start talking about life paths and how he wasn't what she wanted—so she added quickly, "Just for tonight."

His eyes flared with a heat so intense she caught her breath. "Are you sure?" he asked, his expression full of lust and hope.

"Absolutely." For once, she was.

"I disappear, you know," he warned.

"But you're here now. And you won't disappear tonight."

"We have to be clear about what we're doing."

"Clear, schmear," she said, still channeling Kitty. "You're always talking about living in the moment, right? The moment's all we really have?"

"Yeah, but...you're not like that."

"I'm willing to try something new. Unlike some people." She jutted her chin at him.

He smiled, then chuckled. "You don't give up, do you?"

"Not this time," she said, and, silently thanking Kitty for the inspiration, she leaned over and kissed his warm, welcome mouth.

He kissed her back, fiercely and quick, then spoke

into the hair above her ear. "Let's blow this pop stand."

So they did. And all the way home on the bus, they made out like maniacs. At her stop, Claire grasped Trip's hand and led him off the bus, her heart pounding, her body aching, her mind racing.

TRIP COULD BARELY WALK for the erection Claire had given him on the bus, where they'd been all over each other like just-released prisoners. Now his desire for her was a drum beat in his head. He had to hold her, kiss her, feel her tight and lovely body naked against his own.

He looked at her face, her chin at a determined angle, her eyes a little nervous. He didn't want to hurt her. Ever. He had tried to be clear...

Clear, schmear, she'd said. Who was he kidding? He wasn't clear about any of the feelings that rushed through him whenever he touched Claire or kissed her or even looked at her. Look what she'd already made him do. He'd bought a watch just to keep track of when he could see her. He'd entertained her office crowd like a trained monkey. He'd written a song for her, even agreed to be in a television commercial to make her happy. And now he was speculating about the truth of Erik Terrifik's claim about the joys of a steady woman.

What the hell was happening to him?

He'd have to figure it out later. Right now, he would focus all his energy on making love to Claire. For now, that was all he'd think about.

CLAIRE HELD TIGHTLY to Trip's hand as they ran to her building, up the stairs and into the elevator. Her legs were rubbery with excitement and she could hardly breathe for wanting Trip. She'd never been this wild for a guy before.

But during the slow ascension to the fifth floor, Claire's sexual boil cooled to a simmer, and by the time they reached her apartment door, she was nervous. Without the rush of arousal in her veins, she remembered how awkward first times were—there would be clothes to remove and positions to figure out. She might be clumsy or jiggly or awkward. She'd been a bit bloated lately....

She unlocked the door and flipped on the lights. At least Kitty wasn't here to gloat or make things worse. "What can I get you? Coffee or beer? I think we have Corona, Tecate, Heineken and something trendy Kitty buys."

"Come here," he said with a soft chuckle, pulling her into his arms, his eyes hot. "Do *you* want a beer right now?"

"Not really."

"Neither do I." He kissed her softly, nuzzled her neck, then went to work on her zipper.

She should do something—untuck his shirt, maybe? He probably expected her to be good at this. Maybe this wasn't such a good idea. She might be just high on the work excitement.

Trip responded immediately to her tension. He pulled back, studying her. "Second thoughts?"

"Not really. I'm just...I'm nervous, I guess. Kitty might walk in...."

"This is all happening pretty fast," he said. "We haven't even talked about protection."

"I'm on the pill and I'm, um, healthy. It's not that."

"It's that this is crazy, right? Yeah." He cupped her

cheek, his expression intense. "I want to make love to you so bad I can't see straight, Claire. But if you can be sensible, I can be, too."

"Wait a sec," she said, putting her arms around his neck and kissing him. The rush of heat returned stronger than ever.

Trip groaned, then seemed to gather his strength, and backed away a few inches. He cupped her face with both hands, his thumbs on either edge of her mouth, and looked deeply into her eyes. "I make a terrible boyfriend. And I don't want either of us to do something we'll regret. Especially you." He gave her a soft, restrained kiss.

She melted like an ice-cream cone in a hot hand, and Trip looked at her like all he wanted to do was lick her right up.

"We don't want to have regrets. Right," she said, dazed.

"This is for the best," he said, his eyes contradicting the words. He reached behind him and opened the door, then took a backward step out, his gaze still on her.

"Yeah, for the best," she said, stepping forward, leaning on the door he was slowly closing.

"Absolutely," he said, pulling it nearly shut.

She held on to the edge of the door. "For sure."

They stood there, looking at each other through the crack of the door. "I better go," he said, not moving.

"Yeah, you better," she said, not moving, either.

He swallowed hard and with one last reluctant look, shut the door.

Claire gave a mighty groan and banged her forehead gently against the closed door. Her whole body ached for Trip, especially between her legs, where *I want, I want, I want* throbbed like a pulse.

Hell, the only regret she had was letting him leave. That was far worse than any second thoughts she might have after they slept together. And who cared if she jiggled or fumbled. She was going for it, dammit! No pro-con list, no second-guessing her instincts, no consult with the Chickateers—even in her head. She grabbed the doorknob, twisted, felt resistance and tugged.

The door gave and there was Trip, his hand on the knob on his way back in. "I was having regrets," he said.

"Me, too," she said. "Terrible regrets."

Then he grabbed her into his arms and kissed her, sending lust through her in a welcome wave. He walked her backward, his hands all over her and hers all over him. She bumped into the arm of the sofa and let herself fall back, pulling Trip on top of her. Their hands, clumsy with lust, struggled with her jacket, his blazer.

They gave up on the outer garments and Trip pushed her dress up to her waist, while she went for his zipper. Her desire for him was a force she couldn't control and didn't want to. All she wanted was Trip inside her—now. All of him. All the way. Which seemed to be exactly what he had in mind.

She heard something rip—her panty hose—and Trip's fingers brushed her through her panties. She gasped, even as she kept her mouth glued to his. He moved the strip of fabric out of the way and touched her. She squeaked, desperate and electrified. Somehow, her frantic fumbling had managed to free Trip from his pants, and he pushed into her hard—sweet relief from a major itch.

"Oh, thank you," she said, feeling as though if he hadn't gotten inside her right then, she would have burned up or fainted.

He pushed in deep, groaned, pulled out, then pushed in again. "Claire," he whispered, sounding full of longing, even though he had her right there.

She made a grateful, garbled sound, liquid with desire.

He pushed into her again and again. She urged him on with her body, her hips, her hands. They were groaning like starving beasts buried in a feast, trying to swallow each other whole.

They still had their clothes on, except where it counted—mouth and sex. Somewhere in there she banged into the back of the sofa. She was at an angle that made every inch Trip moved enflame her more.

"I'm...coming," she cried, startled by how fast she'd gotten there—no close-but-no-cigar phase, no dragged-out, sweaty struggle to the peak and over.

At her words, Trip thrust into her hard and she felt him release at the instant she started her ride. He gripped her body, holding her as they rocked through the feeling.

When it was over, the world, which had been a distant blur, shimmied slowly into focus.

Panting, Claire became aware that she'd bumped her head on the sofa arm and bruised her shin on something—probably the coffee table. She looked past Trip at the doorway, where she could see the hallway and the neighbor's door. "We left the door open."

He rolled to the side to look out, then back at her.

"Yeah, we did." He grinned, stroking her thigh above where he'd shoved her torn panty hose.

"Anyone could have seen us," she said, wide-eyed.

"Lucky them."

She chuckled, feeling as shameless as he'd sounded. "All I can say is wow."

"You have a way with words."

"I felt almost possessed."

"Isn't that what sex is? The primal urge? An unstoppable drive, the biological imperative."

She put her finger on his lips. "Stop. Don't demystify this for me. If you start talking biology, you'll ruin everything. I don't want to be compared to the rutting rhinoceros."

Trip chuckled. "You're skin's too soft for that." He kissed her gently on the mouth and she felt the heat rise again. "Let's try this with fewer clothes." He reached behind her neck for her zipper.

She gripped his forearms, stopping him. "The door?"

He released her zipper, but made no attempt to move from the couch. Instead he kissed her, slow and warm and intense. "Maybe we could sell tickets to the neighbors," he said, reaching between her legs.

She slapped at his hand. But not very hard. "If we move to a bed there will be less bruising," she said. Still throbbing, she gathered what was left of her good sense and went to lock the door.

Once in Claire's bedroom, they undressed and climbed into bed, lying face-to-face. Trip ran his fingers lightly over the surface of Claire's shoulder, sending goose bumps racing across her skin.

Claire closed her eyes, ready to be swept away.

"Let's take it slow this time," Trip said.

"Huh?" Claire's eyes flew open. "Slow?" She was

practically quivering with anticipation. Going slow would be agony. Plus it would give her time to think, which she did not need right now.

Trip traced her arm down to her elbow, then along the dip of her waist, the curve of her hip... "Yeah," he said, moving down her thigh to her knee. "I want to take time to feel everything." He barely brushed the skin of her belly, then skimmed lower.

"Ohhh," she said, and let her eyes close.

"Tell me what you like, Claire."

"Everything," she said, shivering with goose bumps and desire. "Whatever you do, I'll like."

"You think so?" He said, scooting so their bodies only brushed for brief seconds—her nipples to his chest, his erection to her stomach. "Do you like this?" He kissed her very softly on the mouth.

Her body seemed to dissolve all over the bed. "Yes," she breathed. "I like that."

"How about this?" He rolled her onto her back, gripped her head and kissed her more forcefully, his tongue searching deep. She felt each finger against her scalp. Lust stabbed through her, hard and insistent.

He broke off the kiss.

She panted, then nodded violently. "That, too."

He smiled a lazy smile. "Good."

"What, is this like sex with an optometrist?" she said, fighting arousal to make a smart remark. "'Is it better like this or like this? Like this? Or this?'"

He chuckled. "I want you to be sure of what you want, so I'm sure to give it to you."

"But I like whatever you do," she said, reaching for his shoulders to pull him down to her.

"Okay, how about this?" He barely grazed his lips over hers, then slid away, the tip of his tongue just touching the edge of her mouth, then above her lip, then just under it, his breath a mist, heat vibrating between them. She reached up for him, desperate as an openmouthed baby bird, but he pulled out of reach.

"That I *hate*," she said.

"Good. Now we both know."

"This is what I want," she said, lunging at him so he fell onto his back. She rubbed her body across him. "This I like."

"Oh, me, too," he said.

"So, what do you like?" she asked playfully.

"I like pleasing you," he said, running his hands down her back and cupping her backside. "I like being inside you." He put his fingers there and she gasped. "I like feeling you come, knowing I helped get you there."

"But what else? For you?" she said, not even waiting for his answer before she placed him inside her.

"Oh, that. Yes, that." She began to move, letting him direct her, make love to her with words, telling her how he felt, what he liked, making her aware of every nuance of sensation. It was exquisite, like a guided tour to orgasm—mutual and separate and even multiple, she was pretty sure.

Afterward, she cuddled against Trip's side, propping her chin on his chest. "So how was I?" she asked.

"You tell me," he said, his eyes full of amusement and satisfaction.

"I was great, wasn't I?"

He chuckled. "Absolutely."

"We were amazing together," she said. "What a team. Gold medal in the Sexual Olympics. First time category."

"Any regrets?" he asked, his expression suddenly serious.

She thought for a second. "None," she said. "You?"

"Not so far. There's something about you...I don't know... You make me feel different. I don't want to analyze it. I just like it."

"Good. I don't want to analyze it, either." She snuggled against him, tucking her face into the hollow of his neck.

He tensed, as if he was uneasy having her there. He didn't put his arms around her, either, but that was all right. This was probably new to him, too.

Before long, his breathing slowed and became steady and she knew he was asleep. That meant he would spend the night.

Tonight he'd been emotionally vulnerable to her. This was the Trip he'd hidden even from himself. Maybe all he needed was the right woman. And maybe Trip was the right man for her. Mature like Kyle, but fun-loving, too. Stimulating, interesting, with loads of chemistry. He just might be her perfect man. With a little fine-tuning, of course.

She could help him find reasons to stay. There was work now—the commercial shoot for one thing. B&V didn't use a lot of original talent, but there was some opportunity there. And there were other agencies that needed talent. Also, maybe she could get him a regular gig. Talkers had music now and then. She'd talk to the manager.

She looked at her sleeping lover. She couldn't believe he was in her bed—something she'd fantasized about for weeks. She imagined waking up with him in the morning and sighed with happiness. They would make love, of course. Afterward, she'd make crêpes with Kitty's crêpe maker, and maybe do something creative with her imported strawberries. Something perfect for her perfect lover.

10

WHEN CLAIRE WOKE UP, she was all alone on a bare bed. The sheet, blanket and spread were in a tangled pile on the floor and Trip was just plain gone.

She tried not to panic. Maybe he'd gone out to buy breakfast. But when there was no sign of him in an hour, she knew the truth. He'd disappeared, just like he'd predicted.

She went straight for the freezer. Screw breakfast. She needed ice cream. Except she remembered Kitty and the empty carton. She was in no mood for pickles—tangy or not.

She would walk to Leonard's and hope that a quart remained of the latest shipment of ChocoCherry Rumba Swirl.

She climbed out of bed, picked up the ball of bed covers and buried her face in them. They smelled of her perfume, Trip's soap and their mingled sex smells. Last night had been so wild and wonderful. And so important to their relationship. At least she'd thought so.

I disappear. He'd warned her, all right. He probably crammed all the intimacy he could into the moment—a complete affair in one night. Like instant rice. Ready in one hot night. *Uncle Trip's Instant Affair.* Pretty funny, she thought. If she could laugh about it, maybe she was okay.

Ignoring the knot in her stomach, Claire took a quick

shower and dressed in a pair of cutoffs and a spaghetti-strapped tank top because they felt good on her body. She still felt sensual from the long night of lovemaking. The jeans seam rubbed her nicely down there and the stretchy fabric of her shirt squeezed her nipples deliciously.

She headed downstairs, waved at Mitch the doorman, and set off. She'd eat ice cream, maybe talk with Kitty when she returned in her own postcoital glow. Kitty and Rex must have had goodbye sex, since she hadn't come home last night. Kitty could give her a refresher course on the casual sex attitude. She would be fine.

She headed for Leonard's, enjoying the spring morning. She moved off the sidewalk into the grass, where trees offered cool shade. She loved the way the air lifted the hairs on her bare shoulders and arms, and how sore her legs felt—exercised in the best way.

But there would be no more of that. Trip was gone. Her heart squeezed. Damn it. Why did she always want more than was right there in front of her? She stopped under an orange tree and rested her head on the green-smelling trunk, breathing in the scent of blossoms that filled the trees and were scattered on the ground around her feet. They reminded her of the Heard Museum grounds where she and Trip had had that talk....

Forget it. It's over. Move on. Trip had disappeared.

Except...could it be? She squinted down the street. Was she imagining Trip's long shape, lazy walk, gleaming black hair? And what was he holding? Flowers? Bright yellow with brown centers... Her heart rose.

It *was* Trip. He hadn't run out on her. He'd gone for

brown-eyed Susans. All her earlier hope came flying back, a yo-yo on a string, slamming right back into her heart.

HE WAS SOME KIND of idiot, Trip realized. And a coward. He didn't know which revealed it more—leaving Claire at four in the morning or coming back at ten.

He wasn't the kind of guy who stayed around, but he couldn't quite leave. He'd gone home, played some sappy love songs, taken a shower and found himself heading back after a stop for brown-eyed Susans and ChocoCherry Rumba Swirl.

He recognized Claire's shape and bouncy walk immediately. He walked faster.

She started to run.

So did he.

He was so happy to see her. She made him want...more. More of her, more of this place, more chance to see what could happen. But he didn't have what it took for intimacy, did he? Maybe he could learn something, like Claire had said. Looking at her face, filled with doubt and relief, he wanted to try.

He dropped his sack to the ground and, holding the flowers in one hand, threw his arm around her and held on tight. Her smell washed over him and she had citrus blossoms in her hair, making him think of spring and fresh beginnings. He buried his nose in her neck and hair and never wanted to leave.

"More flowers?" she said, breaking the embrace to take them from him. She held them close to her face, the yellow glow reflected on her cheeks, then looked up at him, full of questions he saw her decide not to ask. "What's in the sack?" she said, looking down at where he'd dropped it on the ground.

"Guess."

"Our favorite?"

"The manager saved me the last quart."

She grinned. "A man of influence in all the right places."

He was tempted to joke back, skip the hard part, but he owed her the truth. "I don't know what I'm doing, Claire," he said, low and quiet. "I know you've had a hard time with men. I don't want to cause you any pain. I feel different with you. But I don't know how long that will last."

She bit her lip, worried but hopeful.

He wanted to promise her more, but didn't dare. He had to be sure she knew the worst of it. "I'm not a guy who runs in place. When the semester ends, I still plan to head for Santa Fe."

"For the novelist...right," she said softly, digging into him with those brown, brown eyes—eyes he could pour himself into. She took a deep breath, as if to steady herself. "How about if we just see how it goes. Isn't that what you said once?"

"Are you sure?"

"I think so.... I'll have more regrets if we quit now. I want to keep going." She gave a rueful laugh. "God, I sound like someone on *Who Wants to Be A Millionaire?* deciding whether to go for the million or stay with five-hundred-thousand."

"And you feel lucky?" he said.

"Very."

He crushed her into his arms, feeling a rush of confidence that he could be what she needed. For long enough.

TWO WEEKS LATER, Claire scooted into Talkers, nervous as hell. She'd convinced Trip to audition for the man-

ager and he'd been hired for a three-weekend engage-
ment. He wasn't that happy about it, but that was
probably because he hadn't been the one to find the
job. Men were defensive about those things.

Emily had insisted they reschedule Game Night to
Friday, so the Chickateers could meet Trip and com-
pare notes.

Tonight was the big night.

Claire could see all three of her friends in place at the
cocktail table closest to the tiny stage. The bar was
packed—the flyers she'd distributed up and down
Central had drawn more than the usual Friday happy-
hour crowd, who were sticking around for the show,
too. She'd invited folks from B&V and Mimi and Georgia were smoking and belly-laughing two tables away.

Ryan had declined—claiming he'd heard enough of
Trip during the rehearsals at New View House. Okay,
so maybe she'd gotten carried away getting everything
perfect—irritating both Trip and Ryan—but it would
all be worth it next Saturday, when the taping went off
without a hitch.

The Greystones were planning to be there. Loralee
believed the whole thing was her idea. *Gag.* But Arthur
Biggs had been emphatic about Claire and Ryan doing
everything they could to please the Greystones. *Stroke
egos, ask opinions, ponder thoughtfully. Just don't go over
budget.*

That was next week. Tonight, she needed the
Chickateers' approval because every day that passed,
she fell deeper in love with Trip. Kitty thought Claire
being with Trip was fine as long as she didn't get too
attached. *He's a traveler*, she'd warned.

She and Kitty hadn't talked much lately. Almost

magically, Kitty had met a guy at the open house the day after their pickle-flavored heart-to-heart and had been spending every spare minute with him.

Claire had tried to keep some distance between her and Trip, just as Kitty suggested, but connections spun between them like cotton candy and she felt bound too tightly to escape without a sticky struggle. Trip was starting to seem like the perfect man for her perfect life. But maybe she was fooling herself.

That's where tonight came in. If the Chickateers approved, she'd know she wasn't crazy to be so smitten. And if they didn't, maybe they'd give her the strength to tone things down.

She headed toward her friends' table, her heart in her throat. "Hey," she said softly.

All three turned to greet her.

"So where's Guitar Guy?" Kitty said as Claire sat between her and Emily.

"He'll be here," she said. "Don't worry."

"Do you think she's going to be okay?" Emily asked Kitty, talking around Claire.

"It's just short-term," Kitty said, doing the same.

"This seems like a bad detour to me," Emily said.

"Would you two quit talking about me like I'm not here," Claire said.

"Are you happy?" Zoe asked from across the table.

"I think so." For now. For as long as it lasted. "Trip is a different kind of person. He challenges me. I like how I am with him. I feel smarter and funnier."

"Sounds like infatuation to me," Emily said. "When you're ready for the real thing, Love-Match-Dot-Com is what you need."

"Those Internet things bring out married guys, sleazeballs and liars, Emily," Kitty said.

"How would you know? Have you tried it?"

"Kitty's not interested because she has Mystery Man," Claire announced to stop Emily and Kitty from a quarrel.

"Mystery Man?" Zoe asked, leaning forward.

"Yes," Claire said. "And he must be really special because she won't talk about him and she won't let me meet him."

"Why? Is he married?" Emily said worriedly.

"Of course not," Kitty said. "We're just madly in lust. No point in dragging him home." Her face was pink and there was a light in her eyes Claire had never seen before. She would not meet Claire's gaze. And all her attempts to probe for info had failed. That was so *not* Kitty, who usually shared sexual details until Claire had to cover her ears and say, "Too much information."

"Come on," Kitty said cheerily. "Tonight the game is Pick Apart Claire's Man—he'll be here any minute so we can really dig in our claws."

"Be nice," Claire said, her stomach jumping.

"Give me his birthday and his full name, and I'll do his numbers for you," Zoe said.

"I don't know his birthday." Or even exactly where he lived. She only knew how much she wanted to be with him and how alive she felt when they were together. "But I know what kind of ice cream he'll want with his cake," she said hopefully.

"I'll ask him when he gets here," Zoe said.

"How's Indiana Brad these days?" Kitty asked Zoe.

"He's really busy," Zoe said, but her whole body slumped.

"He's avoiding you," Kitty declared.

"How's your calligraphy class?" Claire asked quickly.

"It's fun. I started on a poster for Brad, but..." Her eyes welled with tears.

"What is it, sweetie?" Claire said.

"I called him on Saturday and I think there was a woman with him. I'm afraid the bike trip to Mexico is off, too."

"Oh, dear," Claire said, leaning over to hug her.

Kitty patted her back. "That SOB."

"I'm sorry to snivel."

"That's what we're here for," Claire said. "It's a special occasion."

"That does it," Emily said. "I'm setting you up on Love-Match-Dot-Com."

"But I'm in love with Brad," Zoe said.

"You don't need a guy who doesn't have the balls for a clean breakup. With Love Match you can pick and choose. And delete rock climbing idiots period."

"I don't know, Em," she said. But they all knew it was no use arguing with Emily when she was doing something for your own good. Before Emily could press her case further, the door opened, and Claire looked up to see Trip striding toward them. She went liquid inside. "He's here," she said, jumping up to meet him.

He hugged her, then sat in the empty chair she pulled up.

All three friends stared at Trip for a silent beat. Their scrutiny didn't seem to bother him a bit. "So, at last I meet the women who never snivel," he said with a devastating wink.

Zoe managed a watery smile. "Except on special occasions."

"You must be Zoe," he said, reaching to shake her hand.

"How did you know?"

"From Claire's description." He took her in, giving her his full attention. "Are you all right?"

"Just a sniffle," she said, ducking his gaze. "Allergies."

Then Trip nodded at Kitty. "Good to see you." He turned to the remaining Chickateer. "You must be Emily."

Emily nodded, shaking his hand, the queen accepting obeisance, then speared him with her most authoritative look. "Claire tells us you're a philosophy student—sort of—and that you take class from a guitarist in town?"

"That's right," Trip said.

"So, how long do you plan to stay?"

"Don't grill the man," Claire said, perturbed and mortified.

"It's all right," Trip said, putting his arm around her. "For a while," he answered, smiling down at Claire. She caught a little tension in his face.

"We're looking forward to hearing you play," Zoe said before Emily could continue her third degree. "When's your birthday?"

Trip told her and it turned out that he'd met Zoe's favorite astrologer, which pleased her. He knew about custom carpentry, too, which made Emily's ears perk up, since she wanted something done in her guest bath. When he suggested Kitty call his landlord to offer her services because the landlord was angry with her current real estate agent, Kitty was thrilled. Within minutes, Trip had charmed the Chickateers, but once he started playing, they were enchanted.

"He's *sooo* talented," Zoe said, squeezing Claire's knee. "And I can feel a really strong vibe from him."

"You think so?" she said, her heart lifting.

"He has potential," Emily observed.

"He might be the one," Kitty said with surprising optimism.

So the Chickateers approved of Trip. Whew! So did the manager of Talkers, she noticed. He stood at the end of the bar, arms folded, smiling and nodding as his waitresses bustled among busy tables. That meant Trip could have a regular gig. Before long, he'd be so popular they could charge a cover and Trip could bargain for a percentage. This could work out perfectly.

TRIP STARTED the third song, weary to his bones. He wanted Claire to be happy and he was pleased to meet her friends, but the pressure of all she wanted from him had begun to wear him down.

He was so tired of playing that halfway house song over and over at her relentless rehearsals. She'd locked him into this gig for three weekends without even asking him.

His sound had broken through the buzz of conversation, he was glad to note. People were listening, tapping their feet, moving with his rhythm, getting into it. He was good with audiences. It was exhausting, though, and it drained him.

He looked at Claire. She was so beautiful. How could she not know how she stood out in a crowd? She thought she was a boring brown wren when she gleamed like the brightest, most tropical bird.

Most of the time when he was with her, he felt better than he'd ever felt in his life. The basic isolation of existence eased and he felt part of something bigger than himself. Sometimes, especially after they made love, he wondered if maybe Nancy had been wrong about him. Maybe he could connect with a woman—give and receive love and all that romantic stuff idealists thrived on.

Being with Claire, his senses seemed raw. Colors were more vivid, sounds more rich, textures more complex, smells more intense. Probably endorphins at work, of course. Biology at its finest. But, still...

He watched Claire tap her toes, wanting to dance, her gaze bouncing from friend to friend, making sure they were pleased. If only she'd learn to trust herself.

If only she'd trust him—stop trying to shape his life into something she approved of. That made him uneasy and smashed all those warm, dreamy feelings flat. He was afraid he'd never be what she wanted. Not for long, anyway.

She'd asked him to move in with her when he had to leave the guest house. The idea made him feel closed in and trapped. New Mexico was starting to sound better and better.

WHERE THE HELL WAS TRIP?

Everyone was in place for the New View House shoot—Claire, Ryan, the Greystones, the crew from Video Voice and the residents they would film. Everyone except Trip.

The videographer and camera guy were listless, rolling their eyes at Winston's filming suggestions and firing off dirty jokes to pass the time.

Claire's frustration mounted and the twist in her stomach became a half hitch. *Come on, Trip.* Video Voice had only agreed to a half day and expected to use only two hours of it.

Ryan tapped his watch. "Call his cell," he commanded.

"He doesn't have one." Trip didn't approve of cell phones. *What is everybody talking about? World peace? Curing cancer?*

But that was just Trip's way to limit his contact with people. Lately, he said he needed alone time. Alone time? They were in love, for heaven's sake. The idea was to be together, not alone.

The half hitch in her stomach doubled to a whole one. "He must have gotten held up."

"It better be by a mugger, because Biggs will be royally pissed if this doesn't happen. The Greystones are restless."

Had he missed the bus? Not woken up? *Don't let me down, Trip. Please.* She'd reminded him of the time twice. She'd even offered to pick him up in Emily's car, which she'd borrowed for today. What she should have done was insist he spend the night with her so she could have driven him, but he'd wanted to catch up on his sleep, and she hadn't wanted to sound clingy.

Ever since the first night he'd played at Talkers and it had gone so well with the Chickateers, he'd been pulling back. She'd tried to ignore the distance in his eyes and the fact that he'd bought newspapers from several cities or that for the last three nights he'd gone home after making love.

He'd stopped talking about moving in with her, too. He had to go somewhere—his landlord wanted him out right away, according to Kitty, who had a buyer lined up—but he sure wasn't carrying boxes over to her place.

On top of it all, they'd argued last night about a band audition she'd found in the paper. He wanted a break.

A break? He'd had a three-week gig. Big deal.

"I have a meeting and Loralee has her nail appointment," Winston said. "What's the hold up?"

"I'm sure he'll be here any minute," Claire said.

"Let's hope so," he snapped, giving her a taste of the terse businessman underneath the genial partygoer he'd been the night she'd met him.

"This is bad," Ryan said near her ear.

"I know," she said, sweat popping out behind her knees.

"Musicians are such flakes," Ryan muttered.

"Excuse me?"

"It's the artist thing. They think they inhabit an alternate universe without clocks or rent. Plus, there's always a lot of..." He pretended to sip smoke from pinched-together fingers.

"Trip's not like that," she said.

"Get real. The guy goes by 'Trip.'"

"That's his real name. His mother's idea. It's a long story... And he would be here if he could be." Icy anxiety speared her veins. "Maybe we should get the footage of the residents. If we have to, we can do a voice-over and a studio needle-drop."

"Arthur wants what the client wants and the client wants the musician," Ryan said.

Greystone was huffing and shooting glares her way. Sweat now covered Claire's entire body. If she blew this, her name was mud at B&V. *Trip! Get here.*

The videographer moved to them. "Look, this isn't happening and I've got a paying job this afternoon."

"Go ahead," Ryan said. "Sorry for the snafu."

The videographer shrugged and headed off.

"We have ninety more minutes!" Claire said to Ryan.

"The time's too short. Biggs is going to be hot enough about this. He pulled in a favor from these guys and now we've wasted it. Not to mention how pissed Greystone is."

"But—"

"We're cutting our losses," Ryan said. "I'm not hanging either of us out to dry for this." He headed off to smooth the Greystones.

Claire moved to the New View guys, who'd been sitting around trying to act cool about being on TV. They were watching the video guys break down their equipment, looking bereft. "I'm sorry," she said to Julio. "I don't know what happened."

Fifteen minutes after everyone was gone, a bus pulled up a block away and Trip got off. He loped toward her.

She ran toward him, not wanting to have words in front of the New View people still in the carport.

"The bus broke down," he said when they met up. "I'm sorry." He kept moving toward New View House.

"Forget it," she said, pulling his arm to stop him. "It's over. You're two hours late."

"We still have some time. Till noon, right?"

"No, we don't. We can't hold a video crew that's donating time until you get around to arriving." Anger made her shake.

"The replacement bus took a while."

"You could have called me and I would have come to get you. Maybe kept the crew a little longer. But, no. You're above using a cell phone. That would be too convenient." She was being harsh, but she was too angry to care.

"Look, I'm sorry. I didn't think the time was that tight."

"If you'd just spent the night and let me drive you here, none of this would have happened. But you had to have your *alone time*." She put finger quotes around the last words.

"I didn't realize, okay? What do you want me to do now?"

"You've done quite enough, thank you. The client thinks I'm an idiot and so will Biggs and Vega as soon as they hear."

"It was my fault, not yours. Do you want me to explain it to them?"

"No. This was my project. I'm responsible for everything."

"So, what about rescheduling?"

"This was a favor, Trip. If we reschedule, we have to pay the crew. A thousand minimum. I don't have a thousand dollars sitting around. Do you?" Of course he didn't. The man earned a living trimming palm trees and playing on street corners.

"Take it easy," he said, trying to soothe her, but there was an edge to his words.

"Take it easy? All I've worked for has just been flushed and you say *take it easy?* Save your philosophy for someone with the time for it."

"I'm sorry, Claire," he said, trying to pull her into his arms. "How can I make it up to you?"

"You can't," she said, close to crying. "I could lose my job over this."

"They're not going to fire you. They know how good you are. Have more confidence in yourself."

"This was my big thing. The chance to show what I've got. And I blew it. Thanks to you."

"So, I'll get the money together so you can do the shoot again. Somehow." He faltered.

"You'll get the money together? How? A thousand dollars is a hell of a lot of trees to trim." The words tasted as bitter as they sounded. Trip's face paled. She should take it back, but, dammit, she'd blown her reputation and lost her chance to get somewhere at B&V. On top of that, Trip was pulling away from her....

"There's nothing wrong with honest labor," he said, his voice low and serious, edgy with anger.

"I know that," she said. "I'm just upset. You let me down. You let yourself down. This was a chance to make real money with your music. No way will B&V hire you again."

He laughed a humorless laugh. "Thank God. I have no interest in working for B&V. The only reason I even agreed to this was to help you."

"You've certainly done a bang-up job of that."

"You've made your point," he said.

"Okay. I know you didn't mean to be late. But I was trying to help you, too. Don't you see? There are other agencies that hire musicians and songwriters and I could get you work—"

"Forget it," he snapped. "I am who I am, Claire. And I'm fine as is. I don't need you to get me lame gigs or dumbass jingles to write. In fact, if you do, I'll turn them down flat."

Anger sparked at how quickly he dismissed her help. "Why? Because you might actually get ahead? Have some money in your pocket? Does having an income violate your values?"

"If it's not what I want...if it doesn't make me happy, then, yes, it does violate my values."

"What's so damn holy about not knowing where

your next meal is coming from? So, what are you saying? Because I want to get ahead I'm a sellout?"

"You want to get ahead because that's what everyone wants you to do. You stand in the dressing room at Macy's letting people toss their choices for you over the door—your girlfriends, the people at work—and you can't scramble into their outfits fast enough. None of them fit, Claire. Can't you see that? For once in your life, put on your own damn clothes."

She'd never heard Trip yell and his words felt like slaps in her face. "If that's true, then what does that make you? Just one more person tossing me getups over the door. You say, 'be a free thinker, make your own rules,' but only as long as I do what you approve of. Your rules stink, if you ask me—don't settle down, don't count on anyone and, for God's sake, don't let anyone count on you."

"And yours are better?" he asked sharply. "You act like your life is ruined over some thirty-second bit of airtime celebrating a place that's doing fine on its own. This stuff is temporary, Claire. It doesn't matter. It will pass."

"Then what's the point of anything, Trip? At least I tried," she said, near tears. "You don't even try. I don't buy this *experience life, live for the authentic moment* bullshit you dish out. Don't tell me you don't feel lost and alone wandering from city to city like you do. What are you afraid of? That people will expect something from you that you won't give? Loyalty? Devotion? Love?"

She saw that her words had hit home. His usual wry look was gone, replaced by pain and desolation, and his face was pale as chalk. "I never promised you more than I had to give," he said softly.

And she knew with an aching heart that that was true. And with that same aching heart she knew that it wasn't enough.

"So, maybe you're right," she said. "Maybe I have let other people influence me too much. But lately, you're the person I've listened to most. And I've never been unhappier in my life."

He looked at her for a long, quiet moment. "Right," he said on an expelled breath. "Then I guess my work here is done."

They looked at each other for a long moment. Claire took in Trip's handsome body, lean and powerful, his musician's hands, strong and long-fingered, his firm mouth, twisted into a sad smile, and felt her heart say goodbye.

He was letting go, too. She felt the cotton-candy webs between them detach, the lines of electricity deaden, the sensory connections fail. His gaze, still on her face, faded to a vacant dullness, like the eyes of someone dying.

Just like that, they became strangers again. Who was this man and how had she ever thought she was in love with him?

"I did love you, Claire," Trip said, reading her mind. "More than I thought I could love anyone. I went as far as I could."

And she knew it was true.

He jolted forward and hugged her—as if he had to touch her just to go on. The smell and feel and heat of him flooded her with sensory memories—the sight of the bright brown-eyed Susans, the scent of citrus blossoms and patchouli, the sound of Trip playing guitar, the touch of his fingers on her skin, even the taste of chocolate mint.

Oh, Trip.

"Goodbye, Claire," he said, backing away.

Panic surged through her. *Wait. Don't go. Let's talk this through.* "I c-can give you a ride somewhere," she stammered, wanting to prolong the moment, stop the pain.

"I don't really have any place to be right now," he said with a sad smile. "Have a nice life, Claire."

He would go to New Mexico, she knew, for the novelist. And then to the Hopi reservation. And then, probably, California. Wine country. She'd seen the brochure in his guitar case. *He's a traveler.* Kitty had been right about that.

He turned and walked away. Claire stood on the sidewalk a block from New View House for a long, long moment, waiting for him to look back at her. With regret? With a last goodbye? A desire to try again?

But he never hesitated. He left without a backward glance. Anger flared. Okay, if he could be that way, so could she. Claire straightened her shoulders, turned and marched back to Emily's car, tears clogging her throat.

Better to know now, before she got too attached. Too bad she'd had to learn the truth in such a career-wrecking way, but maybe that was what it took to slap sense into her.

She started the drive home, blinking back tears— about Trip and about her career. Arthur Biggs's words came back to her: *Just don't make me regret this, Claire....* That's exactly what she'd done, and she felt sick about it.

Okay, she thought, gripping the wheel. *You can fix this, Claire.* What would Ryan do? Something clever and tricky, no doubt. But Claire wasn't like that. She was direct and honest. And she intended to stay that way.

On Monday, she'd go straight to Biggs's office, take full responsibility for the fiasco and offer to do whatever she could to make up for her mistake. It wouldn't be pleasant, but it would be clear and straightforward.

She relaxed a little and settled in for the drive home. Except just then Emily's Volvo sputtered and died. She'd let it run out of gas again. Instantly, she thought of Trip saving her with the yard guys' gas, and burst into tears.

She banged her head on the steering wheel. The horn sounded. She'd forgotten it was there. So much for learning from her mistakes.

Resolutely, she locked up the car and started for the gas station down the road. A man stopped to offer help, but she turned him down. This time, she'd damn well rescue herself.

11

BY THE TIME she got home, Claire had concluded that breaking up was for the best. Her instincts had been wrong once again. Trip wasn't right for her. And he certainly didn't love her enough. He'd walked away like he was leaving an irritating date, not the love of his life. He'd been right from the beginning, she guessed. They were on different paths. He had no interest at all in taking the merge lane onto hers.

Maybe she did listen to other people's opinions too much, like Trip said, but at least now, in the moment of crisis, she'd been true to herself. She cared about her work—about B&V and about New View. She wanted to make a difference, to work hard and succeed. And Trip couldn't make her ashamed of that.

His philosophy was a smoke screen behind which he hid from commitments and obligations and connections. She could never live like that.

She was proud of herself for that truth, despite the pain of knowing she'd done it again—fallen for a man she couldn't have. He wasn't married, like Jared, but he was just as unavailable. Emotionally, this time.

She'd like to talk to the Chickateers. She could schedule an emergency Game Night, but weekends were "Barry time" for Emily, Kitty was spending the weekend with her secret lover and Zoe's new belly-dancing class was on Saturday afternoons.

So, Claire was on her own for emotional first aid. She pulled up to her corner, fighting the faint hope that Trip would be waiting on the steps with a bouquet of forgive-me brown-eyed Susans, promising to turn over a new leaf. But the only person on the corner was the yard guy blowing grass clippings into the gutter. Mitch the doorman wasn't even at the security desk to give her his usual cheery greeting.

Claire headed up the elevator and down the hall and put her key in her apartment door. Kitty was off with Mystery Man, so she'd have the place to herself at least.

Except she opened the door and was amazed to find two naked people asleep in spoons position on the zebra-striped sofa, their clothes strewn on the floor.

Kitty and, of all people, Kyle Carson.

Claire's gasp woke the sleepers. "God!" Kyle said, then grabbed a leopard-spotted pillow and tried to cover Kitty's bare bottom.

"Claire!" Kitty said, jerking to a sit, exposing Kyle's nudity. He clutched the pillow over his groin, grabbed Kitty's blouse from the floor and held it in front of her.

"Wow," Claire said.

"I can explain," Kitty said, slipping her arms through the sleeves and clutching the blouse closed.

"You don't have to," Claire said, stunned. Kyle and Kitty? How had this happened? They'd only met that one time....

"Kyle was the guy at the open house," Kitty said.

"Interest rates are down," Kyle interrupted, handing Kitty her shorts. "It's a buyer's market. And I saw Kitty there in the doorway, and it was—"

"—Such a funny coincidence," Kitty finished for him, struggling into her shorts. "So we went for coffee."

"Just coffee," Kyle said, looking ridiculous with the pillow over his crotch. He had a purple hickey on his neck and his painfully neat hair was rumpled. He looked cuter than she'd ever seen him.

"We hit it off," Kitty said, her eyes pleading with Claire. "Can you believe it? I mean, look at him, he's such a nerd."

"Yeah, I'm such a nerd," Kyle said. "I never dreamed she'd see anything in me."

"I told him I couldn't go out with him...because of you, Claire," Kitty said.

"But I told her you and I had decided to just be friends," Kyle said.

"But I was still afraid you'd be upset," Kitty said. "Plus, I thought this would fizzle. I mean, what are the chances we would stick?"

"A million to one," Kyle said.

"A trillion," Kitty added.

"Let's not get carried away," Kyle said with a frown.

"Whatever. The fact is, here we are," she looked at Kyle with love and misery, then at Claire. "I knew I had to tell you soon and—"

"Hold on," Claire said, raising her hands to stop the onslaught of overlapping defenses. "It's all right. Really. I'm happy for you. It's just a surprise."

Kitty and Kyle. Talk about a mismatch. Except, now that she thought about it, maybe not. Kyle had been looking for a jolt. And Kitty probably needed somebody stable to ground her. Hell, even their names sounded good together. Kitty and Kyle. Kyle and Kitty.

"I know, Claire," Kitty said. "And if this hurts our relationship, I don't know what I'll do." She climbed off the couch and moved closer to Claire, her face full of despair.

"I'll let you two talk this out," Kyle said, standing and clutching the pillow over his parts. His whole body was blotchy with blush, except for the hickeys. There was another one above his left nipple and one on his kneecap. Huh? His kneecap? "Whatever you decide to do about us, Kitty, I'll agree to." He snatched his pants and shirt from the back of the sofa and backed out of the room.

"Are you mad at me?" Kitty asked Claire, toying with her misbuttoned blouse.

"Of course not. I'm not mad." She was still a little shocked, but Kitty's concern touched her.

"He's like a drug to me," Kitty whispered. "He's so...straight...so boring...but I can't get enough of him. What's wrong with me?" She looked desperate. And deliriously happy.

Claire smiled. "There's nothing wrong with you, Kitty. You're in love."

"You think so?" That didn't seem to make her feel any better. "And you're not mad at me?" she asked in a small voice.

"I'm a little hurt that you didn't trust me enough to tell me, but I understand. And maybe I'm a little envious that you've found someone...."

"But you have Trip," Kitty said. "We both have someone."

"Not anymore," she said, the pain welling up her like a snapped-off water sprinkler. "We just broke up."

"Oh, honey, I'm so sorry," Kitty said, pulling her into a rough hug as Claire began to cry.

Kitty joined in.

"What are you crying about?" Claire said through her tears, pushing away from Kitty. "You're in love."

"Yeah, but I'm scared I'll screw it up."

They were still crying when Kyle returned, his shirt buttoned as badly as Kitty's, his tie askew, his shirttail sticking through his zipper. "I'm sorry," he said glumly. "If you need to break up, Kitty, I understand completely. Friendship is too important to risk."

"Oh, shut up, you big goof," Kitty said to him, smiling through her tears. "We're not crying about that."

"What then?"

"Claire's crying because she broke up with Trip. And I'm just scared."

"Come here," Kyle said and opened his arms to Kitty.

She went to him, looking like she belonged there. This was a Kitty Claire had never seen before, her hard-shell finish dissolving like beeswax in a saucepan.

"I'm sorry about Trip," Kyle said over Kitty's shoulder.

"It had to happen," Claire replied, her heart aching. "And I'm happy for you two."

"We'll pay rent until you can find a new roommate," Kyle said, "but I'd like her to move in with me as soon as possible."

"Move in?" Claire asked.

Kitty pulled out of Kyle's embrace and faced Claire. "Kyle thinks living together will help us."

"You're moving out?" Claire said numbly. "But you've only been here two months and we were having so much...fun." Claire seemed to be losing everything at once.

"We can still have fun. We have Game Night and you and I will hang out more now that you know about Mystery Man." She looked lovingly at Kyle.

The last thing Claire wanted was to be the third

wheel on that bicycle. "Sure," she said. "That'll be great."

"And you can keep my furniture. It doesn't go with Kyle's stuff anyway."

"Thanks," she said. With a sinking heart, Claire realized that except for the sex den decor, she was back where she'd started the day of the K-BUZ call that had changed everything. She had an apartment she couldn't afford, a dead-end job and no boyfriend.

Except now she was worse off. What she felt for Trip was real love, not the false in-love-with-love thing she'd had for Jared. Her pain wouldn't be soothed by sharing a carton of ice cream with a sexy stranger. And on Monday, she might not even have a job, dead-end or not. She'd put her heart and job on the line and lost both. Her perfect life had been shot to hell.

"You know," Kitty said, tapping her nail on her lip, "I think that female impersonator I used to room with needs a place. He's such a good designer and he gets great furniture discounts. Want me to call him?"

"No, thanks," Claire said sadly. "I'm not up for show tunes right now." And, judging from how miserable she felt, maybe never again.

TRIP LEANED BACK in the overstuffed leather chair where he sat in a semicircle of aspiring writers around the famous novelist, behind whom crackled a mesquite-wood fire, and tried to focus on the wisdom the man had to offer. "Write what you know," the novelist said soberly, as if delivering the stone tablets.

Trip's gaze kept falling on a woman in the group who had the same upturned nose as Claire and almost the same color eyes. She was taking down every word the man said. Claire would be a copious note-taker, too, he was sure.

"This doesn't discount the value of research," the novelist continued in his pretentious drone.

Why had he come here? Trip asked himself. To explore his own vision, to deepen his ability to find and tell powerful stories, to enjoy the particularly crisp, bright light and air of Santa Fe's high desert.

To get away from Claire and all he felt for her.

Standing there, fighting with her on the sidewalk, he'd felt his happiness slide away like sand in an hourglass.

And he'd just let it go. Why?

She scared him. She expected things from him. Things he couldn't offer—commitment, dependability, staying in one place. She wanted him to love her for better or worse, in sickness and in health and all that corny lunacy.

That wasn't him. He moved freely through the world. He didn't put down roots and get stuck, build walls against experience or close doors to choices. Worse, he didn't have the emotional equipment required to do any of it. He'd known that since high school. He'd tried to stretch, for Claire's sake, but it had been an illusion.

Just for a moment, though, during their argument, he'd wanted to say, *You're right. I'm scared shitless to let something count, to make it mean something. I can't bear the hurt of it not working.*

But in the end he'd returned to what he knew about himself. He had to stay independent, self-sufficient and flexible. Claire had confused him. Her open heart and her earnest soul had bewitched him. He couldn't bear to see her face when he disappointed her, which he inevitably would.

Focus, he told himself, adjusting his position in the squeaky leather chair. Focus on what? A pompous ass who'd ended up on the *New York Times* bestseller list only because his mediocre novel's release coincided with a resurgence of Southwestern chic?

On the other hand, even Hemingway wouldn't be able to distract Trip from the pain he was feeling right now. He could still hear her voice in his head—sometimes yelling at him in their fight, but more often eagerly describing some ad she was working on, or laughing with her face tipped up, or moaning when she spooned down ice cream, or crying out in sexual pleasure.

Claire.

"SO, LOOKS LIKE I'm sniveling again," Claire said on the following Game Night, letting out a shaky breath. "Right back where I was before Valentine's Day. Square one. Make that square minus one."

She'd told the Chickateers the story of the ruined ad shoot, the breakup with Trip and her awkward status at B&V. She hadn't gotten fired, but Ryan was pissed and Biggs terse. She'd let down the firm. She felt lucky to keep her sad little accounts and Mr. Tires was feeling neglected since she'd spent so much time on the New View House project.

"Just let it out," Zoe said. "Breathe out sorrow, breathe in hope...from your diaphragm." Zoe demonstrated, but her heart didn't seem to be in it. Something was bothering her...and the other Chickateers, now that Claire looked up from her own misery long enough to notice. Kitty was irritable—having second thoughts about moving in with Kyle, she knew—and Emily seemed bossier than usual.

"Enough with the deep breathing, already." Emily rolled her eyes. "You have to breathe. Doing it some special way doesn't solve anything. Trip was just your transition relationship, Claire. Now you're ready for the real thing."

"This felt pretty real to me," Claire said. "It's your turn, Kitty."

Kitty rolled the dice, counted, then said, "Sorry," and moved Claire's game piece backward to the beginning of the slide. The game for tonight was Sorry! and Kitty had chosen it as a way to apologize for keeping Kyle secret and for moving out...and because she was sorry she'd fallen in love in the first place, Claire guessed.

The game was perfect for Claire's situation, too, since it consisted of moving merrily ahead, making dogged progress, only to be pushed back half the game by another player's move.

She didn't really care about the game tonight, though. She needed her friends to help her decide what to do next. The pain of breaking up with Trip had gotten worse every day.

"I've got your solution right here." Emily reached into her purse and pulled out a folded paper, which she handed over. "From Love-Match-Dot-Com. I printed out a sample guy."

Kitty leaned over Claire's shoulder and looked with her at a man's photo with his bio, job, hobbies and interests. He was attractive, but his quote said, "I enjoy sunset walks in the desert, tabby cats and the chocolate soufflé at Roy's Pacific Rim." Completely hokey. But even if he'd seemed perfect, Claire had no interest whatsoever. "Too soon," she said, handing Mr. Tabby's dossier back to Emily.

"She needs to grieve," Zoe said.

"Grieve, schmieve," Emily said. "She'd barely kicked Jared out before she went for Trip. And if people spent half the time looking for a mate that they spend choosing a career, there wouldn't be so many women with nothing but Siamese cats and soap operas to keep them warm." She slid the paper back to Claire.

Zoe shook her head. "You have to have faith. Send out your energy and when the time's right, he'll be there."

"That's nutso," Emily said irritably—too irritably, Claire thought. "I've got one for you, too, Zoe." She handed another sheet across the table—Santa passing out goodies from his pack.

"Quit telling Zoe and Claire what to do, Emily," Kitty snapped.

"I'm saving them time," Emily said, startled by Kitty's tone, which was harsher than usual.

"No, you're not. You're controlling them. Trying to turn them into your clones. Everything's always your way. Even with the games. It's always Emily's rules." Her voice rose with overblown anger. "What Emily says goes. Always."

"Kitty!" Zoe said, sounding shocked.

Emily's lips went pale. "You are such a bitch, Kitty."

"Yeah, I'm a bitch, but at least I'm honest about it. You pretend you're bitchy for our own good."

"You're just jealous because you can't find a husband." Emily's voice held an uncharacteristic wobble.

"I'm jealous? Of what, Barry the Valance Master?"

"Kitty doesn't mean that," Zoe said. "Her opinions are just fierce sometimes."

"Oh, yes, I do mean it," Kitty said. "And you should quit letting Emily push you around, Zoe. Quit being a wimp. You let her talk you out of Indiana Brad. Just call the guy. Take charge of what you want for a change."

"I do my best," Zoe said, sounding wounded.

"Of course you do," Claire said. "Take it easy, Kitty."

"If this is how you behave when you're in love," Emily said to Kitty, "I liked you better when you were sleeping around."

"Sleeping around?" Kitty's face went red. "You mean getting some? Which you don't. You're the one who's jealous, Emily. You chose Barry. Live with your choice. Don't expect us to approve of it."

"At least I made a choice," Emily said. "You're about to blow it with Kyle because you're scared. Barry may not be the most handsome or ambitious or clever." She gulped. "Maybe he is a loser, but he's my loser. And he loves me." She choked up. "At least he used to." And then her face crumpled into tears.

Claire, Zoe and Kitty looked at each other, startled. Emily never cried. Ever.

"What's wrong?" Claire said, trying to hug Emily, who remained ramrod straight, tears streaming down her face.

"I'm sorry, Em," Kitty said, reaching to grab her forearm. "I'm just freaked about Kyle. And that makes me more of a bitch than usual, I guess, and—"

"Oh, shut up, Kitty," Emily said, extracting her arm from Kitty's bruising grip. "I'm not crying over what you said. I'm pregnant and Barry won't speak to me."

"You're pregnant? Oh, congratulations," Zoe said

uncertainly, since Emily's face was red with sadness and wet with tears.

"This is supposed to be the happiest time of my life and I'm miserable. Barry's not ready."

"But you talked about it, right?" Claire asked.

"Yes, and we agreed that this is the right time."

"You mean you *told* him it was the right time," Kitty said.

Emily glared at her.

"Sorry. I just know you."

"I thought it would take a while to get pregnant, but it worked the first time out."

"You've always been very efficient," Zoe said.

"I know. But my ovaries, too?"

"He'll come around," Kitty said. "Men don't like change. If a pair of briefs lands on the coffee table, that's where a man thinks it belongs."

"He hasn't spoken to me for a week," Emily said. "He's never sulked this long before. I knew when I married him he was immature, but I thought he'd grown up enough for this."

"Oh, Emily," Zoe said. "I'm so sorry."

"I know you are," Emily said, reaching across to squeeze the hand Zoe had extended. "And I just wanted to help you and Claire with the Internet thing. I don't want to make clones." She shot Kitty a look.

"Yeah," Kitty mumbled. "I know that."

"It feels like everything I've worked so hard to build just collapsed like...like..."

"A pile of Pick-Up Stix?" Kitty offered.

Emily managed a wan smile.

"A hand of poker?" Claire threw out.

"A Jenga tower?" Zoe chimed in.

"All of the above," Emily said.

They all smiled sadly at each other, then focused on Emily.

"Barry will come around," Claire said. "And in the meantime, we're here. Your baby's three aunties. You can show us baby gear and we'll ooh and ah like crazy."

"Oh, yeah. I like critiquing baby clothes much better than valances," Kitty said, rolling her eyes.

"All for one," Zoe called out, holding up her wineglass in trembling fingers.

The friends lifted their goblets and faintly chorused, "And one for all. No sniveling." And then they proceeded to snivel, each in turn, until the waiters started upending the bar stools.

CLAIRE WALKED HOME from Game Night with a lot on her mind. The Emily-Kitty quarrel had opened up some frank talk between the four, who had been smoothing over some resentments and worries for the sake of staying upbeat.

Opinions varied about their respective problems. Claire and Zoe thought marriage counseling would be good for Emily and Barry, an idea Emily dismissed. Zoe had to decide whether or not she really loved Indiana Brad and, if so, figure out how to lay her heart on the line without risking her body on the rocks.

Kitty had more or less agreed that the next time she was tempted to pick a fight with Kyle just to test his love, she'd call one of the Chickateers first.

Claire was on her own. She'd gone to Game Night wanting the Chickateers to tell her what to do, but halfway through the evening, she realized she didn't want that. She had to search her own heart. She was the one who had to approve of her life. Just like Trip had said. Okay, so he was right about that.

She felt better because of Game Night, though— buoyed and strengthened by the warmth of her friends' love and support. She still ached for Trip, and her career was still in shambles, but she had friends who'd be there for her. And that was damn near perfect.

Reaching her corner, she checked for Trip, as she had every day since the breakup. He wasn't there, of course. But upstairs, her answering machine was blinking and her heart leaped to her throat. She rushed to the machine and hit Play.

"Claire, hey," said a familiar voice. "I've been trying to catch you, but I guess I'll have to settle for the machine."

It was Jared. She froze, listening.

"I did it, Claire. I told Lindi I want a divorce. She claimed she had a miscarriage, but I think it was a lie. I'm through being jerked around." He blew out a breath, then seemed to collect himself. "The point is that I'm free and I want to see you. I miss what we had. Call me."

For a flicker of a second, Claire felt triumph. Jared had given up his marriage for her. Everything she'd wanted two months ago could be hers.

But she didn't want that anymore. Not even close. She hadn't loved Jared. She'd been trying love on for size. It was completely clear to her now. She didn't need to test the truth of it with the Chickateers or anyone else.

She *had* loved Trip. Still did. Of that she was certain. Maybe he'd been wrong for her, but she loved him. She trusted herself to know that. And from now on, she would trust herself on the important things. From now on she would stand on solid ground in her own bare feet, not somebody else's wobbly heels.

She'd learned that from being with Trip, from falling in love with him and from thinking about what he'd said to her. Not all his philosophy had been bogus. *You have no idea how good you are.* That's what he'd said about her at work.

He was right. And she realized something else. She wasn't finished with the New View House ad. Her idea had been solid—before Trip came along with his song. She should have insisted they get footage the moment it was obvious Trip would be late. Instead, she'd let Ryan decide.

She thought about Ryan. She used to believe he knew more, was smarter and more talented than she. But all he had was more experience and an ability to make things look better than they were.

She'd asked him to be her mentor, thinking she needed him to get ahead, but everything she'd achieved she'd done on her own. She'd volunteered to take over the New View House campaign. She'd led the creative team. She was the one who'd successfully pitched the PSA to Arthur and the Greystones. Of course, Trip's song had been the linchpin, but that didn't negate her part in the success.

She'd been leaning on Ryan's opinion about her career, just as she'd leaned on the Chickateers' advice in her personal life. Ryan knew how to look good. Claire knew how to *be* good. So that was what she'd do.

She didn't have money to pay for a videographer, but she could contact the film department at ASU, see about a graduate student who needed a project for his portfolio. She'd make it happen. All on her own.

She *was* better than she thought she was.

12

TRIP SMILED while the writers sliced and diced the short story he'd presented to the group for critique. *Sentimental. Cliché-ridden. Suitable for a confessions magazine.* He should be utterly humiliated to see his work trashed, but he knew they were right. And he wanted to laugh out loud.

He'd set out to craft a story about the intellectual challenge of finding happiness in a world bent on overstimulation and immediate gratification, but it had turned out to be about how he'd felt with Claire, the way she made him want to be more, do more.

When he was with her, he'd felt like he had before his mother got messed up—and with the family in Fresno, too—safe, able to rest, to put his weight down, dig in and be home.

Before Claire, he would have called that false security. Home only existed when you had peace of mind. Except now his peace of mind seemed to require Claire.

"Do you have any questions for Trip?" the blowhard novelist asked the circle of earnest critiquers.

"Can you explain your thesis?" asked a woman who'd flirted with Trip for the past two weeks, despite his unresponsiveness. She leaned forward, waiting.

"My thesis?" he repeated, managing a self-mocking smile. "Isn't it obvious? Love gives life meaning."

The students looked at each other, their expressions eloquent: *What is this guy doing here?*

Trip wondered the same thing.

The workshop ended for the afternoon, and Trip moved through the milling crowd between campus buildings. Then he saw her—a woman searching faces, then turning away. It was Claire. He knew it. Had she followed him here? What a crazy, insane thing to do—a perfectly Claire thing to do.

He hurried after her, pushing through the crowd. "Hey," a guy said when he bumped him. "Watch it," said another when he pushed past. The woman started across the parking lot. He tripped over a leg, caught himself on the hood of a car, then shouted at the woman, "Wait!"

She turned, but it wasn't Claire. The face was more narrow, the eyes not as earnest, the mouth not so sweet.

"Sorry," he said. "I thought you were someone I knew."

She smiled. *We can fix that*, her expression said.

He didn't want to fix it. He wanted Claire.

But that was impossible. He wasn't what she wanted or needed. Going back to her wouldn't be fair to her. He just had to get over this ache in his gut, this hollow feeling in his chest.

Head down, he walked back to his room in student housing, sat on his bed and pulled out his guitar. A song had been playing in his head. A sweet tune, with sharp highs and whimsical runs. He pushed away the phrase that kept popping up. My Claire...my sweet Claire.

It must be time to move on. Sure the air here was crisp, the light nice. But the writing had been a bust. He felt more like making music. There were coffeehouses all over northern California and the Northwest. That's where he'd head.

He tried to make the song philosophical, about how love means loss and learning and moving on, but it kept being about going home.

A WEEK LATER, Trip was washing dishes at the restaurant down the block from a bus station. He'd almost earned the fare to San Francisco, but all he could think of was Claire.

"Sugar, you're washing the color right off them plates," the fortyish waitress said. Her eyes were weary, her smile sad. Her second husband had just left her, Trip had learned when they were cleaning up the night before. "Why don't you just do it?"

"Do what?" He stopped scrubbing and looked at her.

"Go to her. You got that hangdog-woman-trouble look. Do whatever she wants. Men like you aren't meant to be alone."

"Men like me?"

"Yeah. You got a big heart. You care about people."

"You think so?"

She made a disgusted sound. "I got no time for men too stupid to know their own selves. Go to her. Work it out."

You got a big heart. The words rang in his head. Clear and true. He did have a big heart. Or at least a bigger one than before. Before Claire, who'd filled it up, stretched it out of shape...or maybe into shape.

He'd felt different about people since Claire, too. He felt connected to them—part of the human family instead of just looking over everyone's shoulders. Even a waitress he barely knew could see that about him.

Maybe this feeling would fade.... And maybe it wouldn't. Not if he had Claire to help him hold on to it, build on it. If he could hold on to the feeling, then he could stay, settle in, make a life and a home, like Claire had already made in his heart.

He put down the plate he'd stripped of color, then threw his arms around the sadder-but-wiser waitress and hugged her hard. He felt her smoke-rasped chuckle against his body.

Go to her. Do whatever she wants. What did Claire want? His love. His commitment. He could give her that. And more. If she would still have him.

The money that wouldn't quite buy a bus ticket to San Francisco was just enough for the fare to Phoenix. At the end of his shift, Trip climbed on board and headed home. To Claire.

CLAIRE SLID THE TAPE into the VCR-television in the B&V conference room, her heart in her throat. She'd twisted Arthur's arm for just five minutes before his meeting to show the spot she'd created. He'd agreed...reluctantly.

As if his impatience weren't enough pressure, now she had to present her work to a semicircle of top account execs, including Ryan, whom she hadn't told about the ad.

Getting it done hadn't been easy. Her student videographer had talent, but did not take direction well. It had taken two days just to get the tape she wanted and by the end Claire, the videographer and the residents of New View were gray with exhaustion. Two nights in the university editing room later, she had a rough cut of a spot she was damn proud of.

But would it impress this tough crowd of professionals? *Believe in yourself*. Trip's words rang in her head. She could almost feel his hand at the small of her back in silent support.

She explained the concept and context of the ad to the group, pointed the remote at the VCR and pushed Play.

She watched the faces of her audience as the images she'd practically memorized flashed on the screen. The sound washed over her—snippets of New View House residents' comments overlapping over a background of decent music. It was no "Hands Out," but it did the job. The total effect was of hard men softening, of a fresh start and new hope.

It was good. She knew it. Even if Arthur Biggs didn't like it, she would do what she could to get airtime for it. She knew what she wanted now and she would go for it—without anyone's approval or advice. Well, maybe a little advice, which she would weigh against her own hard-won wisdom.

As the spot played, there were smiles, a hum of approval, a laugh at the right place. And then it closed. *Help make this a home for more… Give to New View House*, with the number to call appearing on the screen under a shot of Julio and Ray with their arms slung across each other's shoulders. Fade to black.

The group applauded lightly while Claire removed the tape from the machine. Arthur asked Ryan to take over the meeting and he walked Claire out of the room. "It's good," he said the instant they were outside the door.

"I'm glad you like it," she said. "I'm pretty pleased."

"We'll need Winston to authorize using Greystone Properties' airtime," Arthur said. "He's a capricious bastard, but he likes New View House. His son lived there for a while, you know."

"No, I didn't know."

"His first wife's kid. Loralee doesn't like to talk about him. We'll see what Winston says."

"I'm sure once he sees it, he'll be convinced. Let me know when and where. Unless you want to make the presentation."

"No. This is your baby." Arthur looked her over, assessing her. "I have to say I'm surprised. After that screwup last month, I figured you'd go back to being a paycheck employee."

"Not me. I want more. And I think I'm ready for it, too."

"You just might be," he said. "Come see me in two weeks. I might have you work on something for Bristol Bay."

"Absolutely. Great."

Arthur hadn't promised her a raise or a promotion or even another account, but he'd been impressed with what she'd done. What *she'd* done, not what Ryan had convinced her to do. She didn't have to try to *look* like a successful ad exec because she *was* a successful ad exec. And, she realized with pride, she hadn't spilled a drop of fluid on the man. On top of everything else, she'd conquered her spillage karma.

If only Trip were here to see this. She'd said that a million times since he'd left a month ago. She wished she could tell him what she'd learned—from him and on her own.

For one thing, she approved of her work. Maybe advertising wouldn't change the world, but it was a place to use her talents. And, who knew, maybe in a year or two she'd get a job at a nonprofit like New View. Not much money there, of course, but money wasn't everything. She would decide what she wanted when she wanted it. And then she'd go and get it.

If only she could get over Trip. They'd loved each other, but not enough. She'd wanted him to be different—which wasn't fair. She'd like to explain, to apologize. To try again, maybe? She hated to think that thought, since it seemed so hopeless. Trip was gone. She wondered if he'd think of her as one of those friends he would visit when he "blew through town."

THE GAME that Wednesday was "Loopin' Louie," featuring a little guy in a tiny plastic biplane. When you hit your flipper, he flew up, then swooped down to knock off another player's circular targets. It was utterly hilarious and Claire had chosen it because somehow, crazily, she'd hit her target, just like that goofy pilot.

All four Chickateers were cheerful tonight. Claire had told about her successful meeting with Winston Greystone, who planned to fund an entire series of New View House ads. Emily reported that Barry himself had suggested a counseling session, which gave her hope, even if the therapy was a bust. Kitty had declared she'd stopped being a bitch-on-wheels to Kyle. And Zoe had told Brad that if he didn't value her for who she was, he could go pound rocks instead of climb them.

"I'm thinking of becoming a therapist," Zoe said now. "I've been reading about psychology, and I realize I have boundary issues, with codependent tendencies, and I—"

"Pleeeez," Kitty said. "I liked you better when you were reading Tarot cards and declaring lucky numbers. Let's toast." She held up her wineglass, which held a spicy, full-bodied Merlot she'd chosen because it reminded her of Kyle. "All for one!" she called out.

"And one for all!" the others answered, tapping glasses one by one, the purple liquid sparkling like jewels. "And no sniveling!"

At least not tonight.

Claire still missed Trip like crazy, but she wouldn't spoil the celebratory feeling of the night. "My turn with Louie?" she asked Kitty, who was sitting across from her.

"Oh, my God, no," Kitty said, her eyes wide.

"So go first, then," Claire said. "You're so competitive."

"No, look." Kitty pointed past Claire's shoulder.

At the same instant, Claire heard the familiar sound of chords strummed the way only a certain person strummed them. She turned and saw Trip sitting on the stool on the tiny stage.

"Trip!" she whispered.

He looked up and smiled at her. Then he spoke into the microphone for the small crowd gathered at cocktail tables. "Here's a new one I just finished. I call it, 'For Claire.'"

It was a beautiful song about believing in love, holding on to it and honoring it. Tears filled Claire's eyes as she listened. Zoe hugged her and Emily and Kitty squeezed her forearms until they'd cut off her circulation.

"I told you I felt forever in your auras," Zoe said.

"That's the first time you've said that, Zoe."

"I didn't want to get our hopes up. Sometimes I'm wrong."

"Not this time, it looks like," Kitty said, sounding wistfully romantic—a new attitude for her.

"Hear him out, Claire," Emily said. "Nobody's perfect."

Trip played to generous applause, his eyes often meeting Claire's. Afterward, he came to their table and the Chickateers greeted him, then excused themselves, leaving arm in arm.

Claire watched them go, her heart full of love for her forever friends, who would always cheer her on—and help her snivel...but only on special occasions.

Trip sat across from her. She should apologize, tell him what she'd figured out about herself and him, but all she could do was stare into his face, which held a light as steady and bright as the spotlight over his head when he'd played.

"I was an idiot," he said softly.

"I'll say." She smiled to show she was teasing.

"Thank God you're still a smart-ass," he said. "That was the first thing I loved about you." He reached across the table and cupped her cheek, the contact so warm and intense that Claire felt like she'd floated off the seat.

"You were right," Trip said. "I was afraid. Afraid I couldn't love you enough, be here for you."

"No, I was wrong. I put pressure on you. I was insecure, too hooked on appearances."

"No, you were right, Claire."

"I was wrong. I—"

He held up his hand to stop her. "I'm giving in here. Could you let me grovel without argument?" He flashed the wry smile she loved and had missed so much.

"Okay, okay." She laughed with joy.

"You made me want more, Claire. You made me believe in love. And in us."

"And you made me believe in myself," she said, her vision blurry with tears. "I shouldn't have doubted you."

"I gave you plenty of reasons," he said, worry dipping his brows. "I know I'm distant and stubborn and difficult. I'm far from the perfect man you want."

"I don't want a perfect man. I want you. I've stopped trying other people's choices on for size."

"I'm glad. You do sound more sure of yourself. That's great. What if you've outgrown me?"

"You never outgrow love, you goof. Love grows with you."

"Oh." Trip swallowed hard, his eyes gleaming with emotion. "When did you get so wise?"

"It started the first time you critiqued my outfit."

Their hands stretched across the table and they gripped each other as if for life itself.

"Don't let go of me," Trip said.

"Never," Claire said. "And I won't push you, either. Trim palm trees, play guitar on corners, wash cars, do dishes. Whatever makes you happy."

"You make me happy, Claire. I didn't think I had what it took to be in love until I met you. Maybe it was being a foster kid, maybe it was my messed-up mother, maybe it was just me, but I always felt like I was broken somehow."

"I'm so sorry you went through all that," she said, aching for the lonely boy Trip had been.

"Don't be. Because look at me now, thanks to you.

I'm in love. I'm not broken anymore. You made me whole, Claire. Or made me see that I already was."

"Oh, Trip," she said, so touched she could barely speak.

"But you'll have to give me time. Staying in one place will be new. And I don't even know what kind of job I can live with."

"Take all the time you want. We have our whole lives," Claire said, and leaned across the table to kiss him. Except she bumped Loopin' Louie's switch and he began to swoop over the game board, knocking targets left and right around them. But they kept kissing, hitting their own personal bull's-eye.

Afterward, they linked arms and walked home, the evening as lovely as the Valentine's Day night when they first kissed. When they reached Claire's corner, she looked up at her place, where she and Trip would make love for the first time in their perfect life together.

Not perfect. Nothing was perfect. But it was right. The right man and the right life for Claire. Something she would build moment by moment, word by word, kiss by loving kiss. She could hardly wait to get upstairs.

Except there was one more thing she wanted. "Play me a song, will you?" she said. "Here on our corner."

Trip knelt, zipped open his guitar case and pulled out his guitar, the streetlight turning the honey wood to gold. He began to play "Hands Out," looking into Claire's eyes, his fingers finding their way along the strings the way he'd found his way to her heart and made it sing.

Two couples in evening clothes approached. They stopped talking to listen while Trip played. When he finished, they applauded and one of the men put a five dollar bill into Trip's guitar case before walking.

Trip picked up the money. "Looks like we can hit Leonard's for some ChocoCherry if you want."

"Uh-uh," Claire said, nabbing the bill and shoving it into her bra. "This is a deposit in the account for your first CD."

"What makes you think I want to make a CD?"

"Well, do you?"

"Maybe. Maybe not." He quirked a brow at her.

"When you figure it out, the money will be there," she said, patting her breast.

"Fair enough," Trip said, pulling her into his arms for a warm kiss that instantly went hot. "Mmm," he said, holding her hips tightly against him. "Got another request for me?"

"A chocolate Santa on Valentine's Day?" she said, feigning innocence.

"You got it. On every Valentine's Day there is," Trip assured her before they hurried upstairs, where Claire told Trip what she wanted and how she wanted it...all night long.

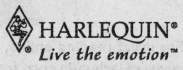

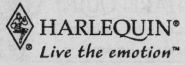

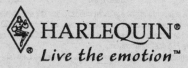

eHARLEQUIN.com

The eHarlequin.com online community is *the* place to share opinions, thoughts and feelings!

- Joining the community is easy, fun and **FREE!**

- Connect with **other romance fans** on our message boards.

- Meet your **favorite authors** without leaving home!

- **Share opinions** on books, movies, celebrities…and *more!*

Here's what our members say:

"I love the friendly and helpful atmosphere filled with support and humor."
—Texanna (eHarlequin.com member)

"Is this the place for me, or what? There is nothing I love more than 'talking' books, especially with fellow readers who are reading the same ones I am."
—Jo Ann (eHarlequin.com member)

Join today by visiting
www.eHarlequin.com!

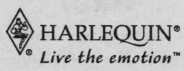